Sylvia Murphy grew up in a family of
middle-class nomads, changing homes
and schools every eighteen months or so
in order to keep pace with a father who
had business interests in the Middle East
and a career in the army during and after
World War II. She left school at the age
of sixteen and received most of her
education later in life. Her several
occupations have included being a
secretary (boring), being married
(difficult), catering (long hours),
publicity (poorly paid) and teaching
(enjoyable but exhausting). She is an
agitator for equality for girls in
education and is also interested in
travelling, sailing, needlework, theatre,
films, carpentry and anything else she
can find the time for. She lives in Exeter.
The Complete Knowledge of Sally Fry is
her first novel.

The Complete Knowledge of Sally Fry

Sylvia Murphy

BLACK SWAN

THE COMPLETE KNOWLEDGE OF SALLY FRY

A BLACK SWAN BOOK 0 552 99094 9

Originally published in Great Britain by
Victor Gollancz Ltd.

PRINTING HISTORY
Victor Gollancz edition published 1983
Black Swan edition published 1984

This book is set in 11/12 pt Mallard

Black Swan Books are published by
Transworld Publishers Ltd.,
Century House, 61–63 Uxbridge Road,
Ealing, London W5 5SA

**Made and printed in Great Britain by the
Guernsey Press Co. Ltd., Guernsey, Channel Islands.**

To my family and friends, to whom none of the people in this story bear even a passing resemblance.

Contents

1 A—Anachronism

A, AN: the indefinite article in the English language. I am sure of this because I can remember learning it at school, and I've often read it when thumbing idly through a dictionary. Why, you may wonder, should anybody want to thumb idly through a dictionary? I've always had a very satisfactory relationship with them. Give me a dictionary any day in a waiting room, instead of a magazine. That's how I came top in all my exams in school. No lateral thinker, no logical analyst, nothing but an encyclopaedic knowledge of trivia because of endless hours in intercourse with dictionaries.

I have to admit, though, that the nature of the indefinite article is not one of the more fascinating pieces of information that has been offered up to me. It has too many illogicalities that yield nothing. Why indefinite, for a start? Indefinite is associated with uncertainty and there's no uncertainty about the rules here. The definite article is 'the', so when you want to refer to a particular something, say a pagoda, it's *the pagoda*, and when you want to refer to any old pagoda it's *a pagoda*. And if you're talking about something that begins with a vowel it's *an* instead of *a*, such as *an igloo* or *an icicle*; unless it's a word like hotel which somehow pretends that the *h* is silent, probably to emphasize the classy French origin, and you say *an 'otel*. This affectation rebounds rather badly, though, if you don't know your Ps and Qs because if you refer to *an 'elicopter* or *an 'ippopotamus* you merely show yourself to be uneducated, or a truly indigent East Londoner and therefore lovable and valuable, which way of looking at it brings forth entirely another set of affectations. It also leads to an example of an interesting *double entendre* possible in the English, 'Have you ever ridden a-n-orse?' which greatly amused Sebastian when he thought of it but did not raise even a smile from his Aunt Julia when she returned from her honeymoon with Sven.

There is a possibility here of introducing AARDVARK, which I believe is some African animal, but as I'm not certain of this I'll go straight on to the next entry.

ABACUS: this is a counting frame used as an aid to mathematics before the invention of adding machines and computers. It consists of rows of coloured beads threaded in tens onto wires; the beads can be moved back and forth to register groups of numbers. I seem to remember seeing a film of some ancient oriental accountant manipulating these beads with terrifying speed so the idea must have been useful to someone but I could never make sense of it. Sebastian was given one for a birthday present when he was rather too young to count anything. He took it to pieces and put the beads in his mouth and I only discovered what he'd done when I saw hideously coloured saliva dribbling down his chin and staining the front of his new T-shirt. I fished the beads out of his mouth and was bitten for my trouble.

My God! I thought. Suppose he's swallowed some!

Motherhood for me has been full of these blind panics. I gathered up as many of the coloured beads as I could find and counted them nearly as quickly as the oriental accountant had, while Sebastian sat and screamed red, blue and green. Have you any idea how many beads there are on a toy abacus? Neither have I. During my third count it occurred to me that any child who was screaming so lustily couldn't be choking to death and poison was the only other hazard. I reasoned that this should be diluted so I gave him a cupful of his favourite drink—that fizzy red stuff that I later discovered probably causes brain damage.

Yes, I know I should have made him sick . . . now.

I didn't worry much about artificial aids to counting until he was fifteen and studying for his GCEs and then I bought him a calculator and he took that to pieces too, during the exam, instead of doing the paper.

'Well,' he said, 'I suddenly didn't see why I should answer their cruddy questions just to prove that I could.' The logic of this remark eluded me then and still does but I have been told that I reacted badly in screaming at him about the cost of the calculator and the cost of the extra coaching he'd had. It's even been hinted that this mercenary point of view may have contributed to his going over the edge, but I have feelings too and I earned the bloody stuff. Anyway, I believe that by that time he was well and truly on his way and not all of it my fault either.

Perhaps I should tell you what I'm doing before I do it any further. My expressed occupation this summer is writing my thesis. Instead of being stuck in a hot and stuffy seminar room taking summer school classes and wrestling with the problems of mature students, keen and demanding at a time when my intellectual drive is beginning to lose its edge, I have taken three months off. So here I am perched on the edge of Cornwall with Mother to take care of the practical problems of life and peace and quiet ahead of me.

It worked out rather well, it being my turn to be with Mother for the summer. She gives her three daughters summer holidays in turn and she was quite prepared to extend the usual month on the grounds that I need her help. She takes a pride in my achievements so it wasn't difficult to foster the idea of renting a cottage in a quiet spot and persuade her that she could contribute to my academic success by dealing with the housekeeping problems. Mother keeps house rather well. Not by cooking and cleaning, you understand, but by organizing other people to do these things, and by having the money

11

to pay them for it. This money is the residue of some family fortune amassed by her grandfather out of the sweat of working brows, and which will never come to me or my sisters because Mother seems intent on spending it all before she dies. In my eager days, fresh with the first flush of social awareness, I used to swear that I would never touch a penny of it, that I would support myself by my own labour. Now I can see that Mother is being quite helpful to society in her own way by providing employment for cooks and cleaning ladies and keeping those old fashioned service-with-a-smile shops in business at the expense of Tesco's and Sainsbury's. I feel quite wistful at the thought of the contribution I could make to the welfare of travel agents and airlines, to say nothing of the good my currency would do spent in underdeveloped countries dependent on their tourist trade.

No, this isn't my thesis.

Faced with a blank piece of paper I suffer from a paralysis of the intellect. On the table beside me is a neat pile of notes and drafts and on the floor I have laid out all the books I brought with me, at great expense considering the extra weight in the car and the library fines. It's all there, ready to go, and I stare at the paper and all I can think about is Sebastian. I could take my mind off him by writing letters but that would only reveal my whereabouts to friends whom I have tried to confuse for the time being. Therefore I shall do the next easiest thing, begin writing my Complete Knowledge.

I've had this idea in my mind for years now. It came out of a pretentious student discussion about whether civilized people could survive on a desert island and someone told the story of the shipwrecked man who decided to occupy his time in writing his own encyclopaedia. When rescue came he had only got to H and he realized that he'd never have time to finish it when he got back to his own life so he said, 'No thank you, I'll take the next boat.' If that's true he may still be there and I wonder how far he's got. Anyway, later I thought why wait for a desert island? This could be fun. Then I thought it could actually be a useful form of self-realization therapy. Does that sound familiar? Perhaps not. You still have to be an ex-student of Bruce's or an ex-client of one of his ex-students, and in proportion to the population that's not yet very many people, to have heard of the Bruce Wild Therapy.

You see, I mentioned the therapeutic idea to Bruce when we were working together at the Uni. Great potential, expanding the consciousness of self, enabling the client to see his problems more clearly: he encouraged me to talk about it, then he began to encourage his students to use it and finally he wrote a thesis about it that earned him his doctorate and his director's post at You-Know-Where. I had no one to blame but myself. How green was my Sally.

Anyway, I learned to play my good ideas close to my chest, and that's not hard with a 32B.

ABHOR: to have a strong dislike or antipathy for someone or something. I abhor Bruce Wild, people who take themselves too seriously, and drug pushers.

I think that's why I couldn't get on in any lasting way with Pope. No, he wasn't a drug pusher, but he did take himself too seriously. At one time I thought it was possible to compromise, to try to take him a little more seriously if only he would laugh at himself sometimes. But he was so keen on telling me that I didn't take anything seriously enough and was so patronizingly encouraging when I did show signs of appreciating him according to his own assessment of his worth. I might have persevered but for Sebastian's conception, which it seemed to me was Pope's first experience of life as it is lived.

'You're going to have an abortion, of course.'

I had been considering this as a sensible possibility but hearing him say it like that made up my mind for me.

13

'I don't see why.'

'I should have thought it obvious. I'm not in a position yet to be the provider of a stable home background and I don't want my children growing up without that.'

'I'm only having one baby.'

'A forced marriage gets off to a bad start and engenders tensions in the family.'

'Who said anything about marriage?'

'Choice of spouse and timing of conception should be considered in a careful and informed manner, not left to chance.'

'Why didn't you tell me that before we started sleeping together?'

'You were supposed to be taking precautions.'

'Nothing's yet been thought of to guarantee against sperms with the tenacity of fifth column guerillas.' It's always seemed to me to be one of fate's cruellest jokes on me that if I'd been born three years later I'd have been able to go on the pill and Sebastian would never have happened. I sometimes suspect Sebastian sees it that way too. Anyhow, when Pope came round the next evening with the name and address of a doctor and more theories about the importance of planning the future generation properly, I exercised my autonomy and decided to become an unmarried mother.

Pope was right of course but since he has pointed this out to me on many occasions since, I haven't been inclined to admit it.

ACCIDENT: something that happens without intention. This follows on very nicely from the above and all I want to add at this stage is that Sebastian's conception wasn't the only accident he was concerned with. He developed a facility for attracting them to himself as he grew up. There is a case for ascribing the misfortunes of 'accident prone' people to a certain level of carelessness in the home, and Sebastian has been exposed to this as much as the average. But I never could see it as my fault

14

that a runaway car catapulted him out of his pram, or a crazed parrot attached its beak to his nose in a pet shop one hot Saturday afternoon, or the school swimming pool ceiling collapsed during the half-hour when he was having his special coaching. Considering the concerted efforts made by the hand of God to eradicate him, the biggest accident of all seems to have been Sebastian's survival so far. Perhaps I shouldn't worry about where he is at the moment. Statistically I can rely on him to reappear unharmed.

ANACHRONISM: something that exists outside its proper place in time.

Mother came in with a glass of sherry and suggested that as I'd been working so hard I might like to relax before dinner. Not that I think sherry before dinner is an anachronism but it makes sense if I explain that Mother had changed from her cotton dress into a silk one, very stylish; had brushed and arranged her silver hair into a shining crown and had changed her single string of pearls (obligatory daytime wear) for a triple choker. No, she didn't have a lorgnette or a parasol but I believe she does possess both these items.

It's my opinion that Mother clings to the manners and accoutrements of a bygone age as a form of perversion. It really would be easier for her to wear casual clothes and look untidy sometimes, but it would also make it more comfortable and familiar for other people and Mother likes to keep people on their toes. I used to try to please her by doing things the way she wanted but I had to give that up when Sebastian's presence in my life became obvious. Then I learned that she was perfectly able to accept other points of view than her own although she would never alter her opinions towards those of others. As, for instance, she knew I would be coming to the dinner table in my jeans and shirt, yet she still changed into her Noël Coward get-up and would every evening as long as we were here.

When she brought me my sherry she sat down gingerly on the edge of the armchair, which I thought looked remarkably clean for a furnished let, and gazed critically around the room.

'I'll get Mrs Pease to give it a going over tomorrow.'

'I thought we had Mrs Barnsley.'

'We do, and Mrs Pease as well from tomorrow. Mrs Barnsley couldn't possibly manage more than the cooking and keeping the kitchen clean. I could see that right away. She's a perfectionist, you see. But she has a friend who'll come in and clean and do the laundry.'

'But Mother, there are only two of us.'

'She's not coming in every day and this is a very big cottage.'

True. It sprawled across its enormous garden like some strange animal spreading its limbs on a hearthrug. Room opened off room and reconnected again in a fairytale network. But still there were only two of us. 'We're not going to use all the rooms. Do we have to keep them cleaned all the time?'

Silly of me to ask. 'It could be avoided, but I would find that uncongenial. Who knows what insects and things might take refuge there?'

But I had to establish a precedent about my workroom. At breakfast this morning I said I would clean it when I wanted it cleaned and then I came up and locked myself in. The initial waves of resentment were almost as overwhelming as a Vulcan mind-meld but I resisted this irresistible force with the dumb strength of an immovable object. Before long the guilt ray moved away and I heard the sound of a vacuum cleaner howling in some distant part of the cottage. Then the car engine started beneath my window and I glanced out furtively to see Mother's Austin driving away, Mother at the wheel fully pearled and hatted, and Mrs Barnsley beside her, equally well dressed, a wide shopping basket on her lap. I wondered why they both had to go and whether Mother might not find it necessary to hire a chauffeur to drive the cook to market. And how long would it take her to find a gardener? Perhaps I ought to suggest it if she doesn't think of it soon herself, and thereby do my bit towards putting more capitalist money into the pockets of the workers.

2   Baal—Bat

Disregarding BAAL and BAALBECK which, like
AARDVARK, I have heard of but know little about, the
logical sequence seems to lead to

BABBLE: incomprehensible talk, such as comes from
infants or drunkards.

Yes, I know I haven't exhausted the possibilities of the
As but unlike the man on the desert island my time is
limited and my purpose is not exactly to fill an eternity of
idleness but to try to come to terms with my problems.

BABY: a newborn or young human being. It does occur to
me that the term 'baby' is also applied to young animals:
baby chimpanzees or baby guinea-pigs, but I'm not certain if this is correct usage. Is there another term for
babies of other species? Is there a more scientific term
for babies of the human species? Not knowing the
answers to these questions doesn't stop them arriving;
the babies, I mean.

My first contact with babydom was the amazing relief
of feeling this wet and slippery thing between my legs
after wrestling for hours with what felt like a gigantic
attack of constipation. Before that day he had been
Foetus, wriggling about and making me tired and giving
me indigestion. Towards the end of his occupancy it had
seemed imperative that he be out soon because space
was at a premium and I had vaguely been looking forward to having a warm and cuddly bundle to fill up the

little woollies and the empty cot. Instead I got Sebastian. The midwife wrapped him up and put him into my arms and I gazed into the hideous little face with the beak of a nose expecting to feel a wave of some emotion called motherhood. But before it had time to dawn he opened his eyes wide and stared into mine with all the penetrating understanding of a Socrates. I could swear that in that first instant of life he made up his mind about everything and found cause to hate me and all the rest of it. Then the eyes closed and he became helpless and mewling. 'Poor little thing,' I murmured and tried to cuddle him close, and thus encountered my first problem. Sebastian was not cuddly. He was thin and very long, with extended limbs that kept popping out of the bundle shape. It was like trying to nurse a spider or a frog. I thought of stocky, thick-set Pope and wondered where this recessive gene had come from. When Mother had fully come to terms with having an illegitimate grandchild she told me he was just like her grandfather, the one who had made all the money. 'In looks, anyway. It's too early to tell about nature yet.'

'If he was demanding and gloomy I think we can promise a good likeness all round.'

'Babies aren't gloomy by nature.'

'This one is.' It rather worried me that Sebastian was two months old and hadn't smiled yet. Then he managed to spite me by giving his first real chuckle to Mother who said triumphantly, 'There you are, all he needs is someone to smile at him!'

Well, I did. I smiled and played and talked and everything I should, and to be fair to Sebastian he did his bit and tried very hard to be patient and amusing and well behaved. It didn't seem to be his fault that he really preferred to sit in quiet corners under tables instead of socializing.

Sebastian had an odd effect on the aspirations of both my sisters concerning motherhood. He made Julia certain that she wanted to produce a child in the proper

19

manner as soon as decently possible, to prove that I had done it all wrong and she could organize her life better. He made Kate quite certain that she never wanted to have any children at all in case any of them turned out like him. Then Kate met Randy Andy, whose nickname wasn't entirely due to a rearrangement of his real name, very quickly became Mrs Randolph, and began producing a succession of pink and white bundles that just popped out like peas and showed that somehow between us Sebastian and I had got the whole thing wrong. Five to date and it's no good telling them that they're being anti-social because they point out that they can make up for the shortfall caused by Julia and me, and anyway there's nothing more social than a young Randolph.

And what happened to the babies Julia was going to have? Well, Julia married Sven, the sexless Swede, and has problems.

BACK: the rear of a person or an object; the part you can't see from the front.

BAD: anything unpleasant that causes distress or difficulty. I suppose that should include anything from downright evil to mildly irritating but I would be inclined to want to express evil in stronger terms. Bad is adequate to deal with life's minor tensions, such as eggs that are too old, inclement weather, children who misbehave, and some of Mother's ideas.

For example, my immediate reaction on hearing that Commander Forrester had invited us over for cocktails and to meet his lady was that this was bad news. Social life with the residents of small villages can become time-consuming and irrelevant, and I'm here to work. But then I thought that sometime during the next three months I might well be so bored with my work, or so well advanced with it, that social intercourse, even with Commanders and their ladies, would seem desirable. Therefore to be churlish now might be counter-productive.

'Who's Commander Forrester?'

'Our neighbour. Over the wall. The one that's too high to see over except from the bathroom window. He approached me in the shop this morning and proffered his invitation. Six this evening.' I had already spied the trim garden next door from the bathroom and wondered if they had an equally good view in reverse.

Mother didn't add 'properly dressed' but I knew of course that she would be, and as Commander Forrester had so far done nothing to offend me (unless you count steering the odd battleship and one can't take that personally), I changed into my Phool shift for the occasion.

They might have been just over the wall but as we couldn't fly we had to trek round a full quarter of a mile of lane to reach their front gate. It was one of those summer evenings that the English survive the winters for and Commander Forrester was sitting on a cedar bench on his bowling-green lawn, chairs and tables set out around him, drinking in the view of sky and sea, and well laced with gin. As we wound our way between the lavender bushes he shouted, 'Hey, Gabby! They're here!' and stood up to shake our hands. He was large and clean shaven with a jutting chin and grey hair swept smoothly back from his face. He reminded me of a large friendly animal but at that moment I couldn't think which one. Then Gabby approached across the lawn carrying a tray laden with glasses, jugs and bottles. When she had put these down on the table she turned and smiled radiantly at us. She was about twenty-five with long black hair, no make-up, a bosom that I envied at once, and she was wearing jeans and a distinctly old sweater.

Of course I thought I'd got it wrong and this was the Commander's daughter that mother had forgotten to mention. But Mother was in control of the situation and said steadily, 'Good afternoon, my dear Mrs Forrester. Allow me to introduce my daughter, Miss Fry.' So I was the only one who was surprised. As we sat down she

21

couldn't quite prevent the corners of her mouth from twitching and I knew she'd done it on purpose.

I was wrong again in seeing Gabriella Forrester as some innocent flattered by the affections of a middle-aged man. She was charming and seductive and worldly wise and she never missed an opportunity to excite her husband by a glance or a touch or a nuance in the conversation. Everything about her made me squirm with envy. It didn't matter that I was both unable and unwilling to contribute to the small talk for the next two hours. Mother and the Commander and Gabby were all entranced by one another and it was enough for me to smile occasionally.

Still in my role as a social appendage I followed the guided tour around the garden, which was quite beautiful and all their own work, down to the little creek where they kept their sailing boat. It was impossible to reach by road and almost invisible from the estuary, we were told, so they were very rarely invaded by tourists which, it seemed, could be a major hazard living in this part of the country. When it was time to go they showed us a wooden door in the dividing wall that led into the back of our summerhouse, which was why we'd missed it.

'There you are! Short cut! Bolt it if you want to keep us out!' The Commander laughed, obviously thinking that the likelihood was remote.

BADGER: a black-and-white nocturnal animal, very handsome but prone to tuberculosis. That's what Commander Forrester reminds me of.

BAFFLE: to puzzle or confound. A lot of things baffle me. For instance, how no one ever noticed about Sebastian.

I admit it's not easy to notice something odd about someone who's never seemed quite normal anyway. To give the school its due, they were perceptive from the start. They referred to him as a quiet, withdrawn child and at that first parents' evening, when I managed to read the teacher's notes upside-down, I saw that they attributed his introversion to his having a one-parent family. This is a text book conclusion and might well have been right, though I would have preferred to attribute it to the fact that Sebastian was totally unlike any case I've ever come across in the literature of disturbance, which is why I was always at a loss as to how to cope with him. But surely it must have become obvious at some point that he just wasn't attending lessons? After the police picked him up in the park one afternoon, stoned out of his mind, I tackled the school about this. They said he was registering in the morning, turning up at some lessons and avoiding those he might not be missed from. They accused him of forging absence notes and of putting up a smoke-screen of confusion as to what his timetable should be. I made a few accusations too. It was one of those large comprehensives with several acres of buildings and dozens of exits and I wanted to know why they hadn't a better system of checking up on their pupils. They murmured things about trust and reliability. What it boiled down to, and what they wouldn't admit, was that he'd been too clever for them.

We got off lightly really. The police were prepared to accept it as a one-off childish prank, though I wasn't so sure about that. The school kept closer tabs on him and Sebastian laughed, actually *laughed*. I had few memories of him laughing and it wasn't a pretty sound. I nearly drowned in shame but I managed to hide it all from Mother and from Bruce, imagining that I was doing Sebastian a favour.

BAG/BAGGAGE: container for the carrying of luggage. Rog and Melly's baggage was amazing.

Melly had a plastic carrier bag with her nightie and a toothbrush and Roger was carrying a medium-sized suitcase containing a pair of pyjamas, some underwear and a complete set of Superman comics dating back three years.

'Did Daddy do your packing?' I wanted to know.

'No. We did it ourselves.'

'Daddy was too busy.'

Rog and Melly? Roger and Amelia Randolph, Kate's second and third children.

I had been battling with my Bs for the third afternoon when the phone rang in the distance. I can always resist telephones and often leave them to ring unanswered, but Mrs Barnsley was in and after a moment's conversation she called me. Mother seemed to be hobnobbing with the Forresters once more. It was Andy on the phone but I hardly recognized the thin voice. 'Sally?'

'Hello Andy, how's things?' That was silly. They must be pretty grim for him to phone in the middle of the day and to want to speak to me in Mother's absence.

'Awful! Kate has to go into hospital today for an emergency operation. My mother will have the baby and the eldest two can stay with the neighbours. Will you and Mother have Melly and Steve?'

I thought very quickly. Steve was still in nappies. Mother wouldn't have anything to do with that and neither would I if I could help it. 'We'll have Rog and Melly here. You can send them on their own on the train, but not Steve. You look after Steve.'

'Me?'

'Why not? He's yours, isn't he? He knows you. It wouldn't be fair to send him away.'

'But I've got too much to do already. Visiting the hospital; work.'

'Andy dear, this is an emergency, isn't it?'

'Of course, or I wouldn't ask you . . .'

'Then take time off work.'

'My boss'll take a dim view of that.'

'Then I'll phone your boss and tell him my view of him. You must be entitled to time off and Stevie needs you.' Andy stammered something servile and incomprehensible. Was it possible that he was frightened of me? 'Put the children on the train in the charge of the guard and then phone us and tell us what time they're arriving at Truro.'

'You'll be there to meet them?'

'Of course. Now tell me what's the matter with Kate.'

'Emergency hysterectomy. The last baby was too much for her. She's hardly stopped bleeding since and this morning she began to haemorrhage.'

So much for them popping out like peas.

By the time I'd broken the news to Mother the children were on the train. Mother's wonderful in an emergency. She telephoned Joan (Mrs Pease was the Rector's sister and the relationship had subtly changed from that of servant and mistress to friends helping each other out). Joan was saving for a family holiday in the Canaries and was only too happy to increase her hours, and to come in at a moment's notice to prepare beds. So Mother organized Joan and Mrs Barnsley (who being a friend of the Rector's sister had been promoted to Nancy at the same time) to cook extra food for dinner. Then she changed into her Truro outfit of linen suit and silk blouse and we arrived at the station with ten minutes to spare.

Rog and Melly had labels tied to them. Their hair was unbrushed and the gleam in their faces was not cleanliness but excitement at this unexpected holiday with Granny by the sea. They leaped out of the train with their inappropriate luggage, waved goodbye to Eddie, the guard, and promptly told us how hungry they were.

'We only had cornflakes for breakfast.'

'What about lunch?'

They exchanged puzzled glances. Rog said, 'I think Daddy must have forgotten about it.'

'We had some money to spend on the train. We had crisps and lemonade . . .'

'And chocolate biscuits.'

As we walked to the car Melly pulled at my arm. 'Daddy will be all right, won't he?'

'I thought it was your Mummy who was ill.'

'Yes, she's gone to hospital, but somehow Daddy

seems iller than Mummy today.'

Another phone call from Andy in the evening told us that the operation had been satisfactory and all that was necessary now for Kate was a period of recovery. All? With five children and Andy to look after that might be wishful thinking.

'They'll keep her in for at least ten days, maybe more,' Andy half sobbed. 'Look, supposing I motor down at the weekend with Steve and Miranda?'

'Suppose you don't. We really don't have time to look after a tribe of children.'

'I must say you're not being very helpful, Sally.'

'I believe in allocating resources sensibly. Surely it would be better if you brought Kate down to stay for a couple of weeks after she gets out of hospital?' That would give us time to get organized.

'Well, all right . . .'

'Give Kate our love. Tell her not to worry.'

I wondered if Mother would have given in to Andy. Probably she would. But she's not the one trying to write a thesis in a house full of children. Of course, that's not the most important consideration under the circumstances, but how else is Andy to learn more about being a father than screwing and signing cheques?

BALLS: spherical objects of various sizes for playing games with. Yes, that sums it up nicely.

BAND: a group of people united in a common purpose; a strip of material in a closed circle—holding the people together, perhaps?

BANDICOOT: someone once told me that there really is such a thing, that they live in Australia. Animals, not people. I've never seen one, not even in a zoo, so I can't be certain.

I have now got through three items without thinking about Sebastian or Mother. That's good, though it

26

surprises me that I should be trying to escape from both Mother and Sebastian. I'm very fond of Mother. She keeps my life together.

A week has passed since the children arrived and so much time has been spent on my real work that the Bruce Wild is being neglected most days. There are a lot of happy noises around me. Joan sings hideously while she vacuums and irons. Rog and Melly spend most of their time out of doors so that their voices have that distant quality which lends such charm to children. They have adopted a young golden retriever which wandered in one afternoon without a collar and which no amount of enquiries could relocate. The helpful village policeman might once have taken care of it, but now that the nearest police station is seven miles away they're not so keen on this local colour and suggested that we might like to take care of the dog until an alternative owner appears. Joey's a friendly sort of animal but very snuffly and bouncy at the wrong times. Late one evening I took him for a long walk to the neighbouring village, left him sitting on the pavement while I slipped into the pub for a drink just on closing time, and left by another door. I was almost home again before I heard a soft padding and slurping sounds that told me I had not escaped. Did I say the children had adopted Joey? Not really. Joey has adopted us: any other view of the situation is self-deception.

I also hear the distant sounds of seagulls, and of a rogue speedboat on the estuary. This sound infuriates the Commander who sees the waters as the preserve of sailing dinghies, and the occasional stately pleasure steamer.

BASTARD: an illegitimate child.

This obviously brings me back to Sebastian but honestly his irregular status has hardly been a factor in either of our lives. The problem has been caring for him and earning a living at the same time, in the early years

27

anyway. Paying for him to be looked after, on top of everything else, on a social worker's salary; and finding time to be with him, with all the other demands on my time; struggling through the crushing emotional defeat of the job together with the knowledge that Sebastian was far more likely to become a delinquent than one of my clients.

The size of the problem came to me one afternoon when I was visiting a client, a nice middle-aged lady whose husband was in prison for pilfering from his employers at a steady but modest rate for over twenty years. As this had been undetected for all that time what he really seemed to be in prison for was getting caught, not pilfering. The wife had taken the whole thing very well really. She almost seemed happy at the thought of having a brief respite from caring for another person and I could quite understand her point of view. But she had been made redundant from her part-time job and needed to claim social security, and had therefore called on me for advice and assistance. As I arrived at her door I remembered that I'd forgotten to make arrangements for Sebastian to be picked up from his music lesson that afternoon. I could remember to look after my clients but I couldn't remember my son's needs. My failure overwhelmed me and I burst into tears just as the door was opened.

'My goodness me,' my client said. 'You need a cup of tea.'

She listened for half an hour and then said, 'You shouldn't be seein' to other people's problems. You got enough of your own. If you ask me you should give up work and live on the dole while you look after your little boy.'

'But I like working more than I like my little boy.'

She shook her head. 'You're stuck with him now, poor little bugger. You got to see it through.' I had already realized this and it was one of the most frightening conclusions I had ever come to. 'Why not go part time, or find an easier job?'

That was why I found myself three months later being interviewed for a lecturer's job at the University by Professor Pope.

Professor!

We had been students together and in the eight years since then he'd done a stint of social work, become a lecturer, written a PhD and got this job. Why him and not me? What had I been doing in the meantime? I felt so inadequate that I nearly blew the interview. But Pope offered me the job and then asked to see Sebastian.

BAT: that's what hit the ball that just came through my window.

3 Bat—Bee

The silence outside was overwhelming. Even the sea-gulls seemed to hold their breath. I picked up the ball from the armchair and hurried downstairs. I passed Joan Pease hurrying up. 'My room,' I said. 'No injuries but a lot of mess.' She nodded and went on. I knew that by the time I returned the clearing up would be almost complete and I wondered if she would be able to resist a little extra dusting while she was about it.

Outside in the front drive sat two quiet figures, arms curled around their knees, heads hanging. Rog's new cricket bat, purchased only yesterday, was laid on the gravel between them. I could swear they never looked up as I approached them and when I stopped they addressed my feet.

'Science,' Rog muttered as I drew breath to rage at them. I wasn't actually angry but I felt that a bit of righteous indignation was in order just to lay it on how stupid they'd been.

'Uh? Science? Science what?'

'It wasn't our fault,' Melly said. 'It happened because of science.'

Rog looked up now, his face bright and eager. 'You know, action and reaction, mass and energy. All combined against us.'

'If you know so much about it couldn't you have calculated your direction and velocity with more accuracy?'

'We did try, but you see Roger's such a rotten bowler and we're only just learning the game.'

Rod nudged her. 'They did tell us not to practise near windows.'

'But we weren't near when we started.'

'You mean the house just sort of crept closer while you were playing?'

'Something like that.' They both brightened up at some sign that I was going to be reasonable about it. They calculated that it was time to change the subject and jumped to their feet. 'Now that you're out, Sally, why not come for a walk with us?'

I made one more feeble attempt to stick to my guns. 'You realize I might have been killed.'

'Oh no, it was only a rubber ball. We certainly wouldn't be so silly as to have used a hard one. The Commander was quite adamant about that.'

'The Commander?'

'You know, Commander Forrester, over the wall? Well, he and Gabby are teaching us to play cricket.'

'He and *Gabby*?'

'She said we could call her Gabby.'

'Okay, but I mean, *she* plays cricket?'

'I'll say she does!'

'She played for England once. That's how she met the Commander, on a tour.'

'And gave it all up to marry him?'

'Oh no, she hasn't given it up. She plays for the village team now. They both do. There's a match on Saturday. Why don't you come?'

At that point Joey came bounding round the corner of the cottage having freed himself from the rope that had been keeping him away from the cricket practice. A walk seemed a good idea.

BAVARIA: a part of Germany. The part where Hitler made his first unsuccessful bid for power, before he learned about manipulating democratic processes. I've never been there but it's associated in my mind with mountains, beer, leather shorts, bright embroidery and princes. Funnily enough, though, I don't see the princes in leather shorts, though I do visualize princesses wearing embroidered ribbons. This seems to me to be a little inconsistent and I wonder if leather shorts were only for the peasants, of which I believe there were many even though during the Reformation they were quite keen on burning them to death if they spoke up for themselves, or if the princes belonged to another historical age before the wearing of leather shorts had become a regional obsession. Perhaps my confusion has something to do with Bavaria being the land from which most of our fairy tales emerged in written form, due to the labours of the Brothers Grimm. The images of romance perpetuated by the illustrations are certainly part of my subconscious and I was aware of the unhealthy potential of this kind of socialization in time to avoid bombarding Sebastian too heavily with that kind of material. I know Mother got in her share of traditional socializing in spite of my vigilance, but on the whole Sebastian's early reading matter was more concerned with travel than fairy tales. Perhaps that's why he turned into a frog instead of a prince.

BEACH: a strip of sand or shingle along the edge of the sea. I could tell you all kinds of facts about how beaches are formed and their subsequent effects upon landscape when they are pushed up or dragged down below sea level. It makes me feel rather insecure to consider that the earth's crust is continually in motion because I can't seem to get the time scale sorted out in my mind in order to reassure myself that a few centimetres in my lifetime will make little difference overall. I know that some movements are more sudden than that, such as Mount St Helen's blowing its belly to the four winds and the erosion of the Essex coast causing people's houses to disappear into the sea a few years after they've bought them thinking that they were fixed for life. These examples point up how silly it would be to decide to live on a receding coastline or near an active volcano. The odd thing is that people do these things quite a lot.

I prefer to think of the beach in relatively stable terms, connected with a walk around or over the headland from our estuary. Yes, already I think of it as ours. There are beautiful golden sands there, within half a mile of the cottage, and if the cricket ball hadn't come through my window I mightn't have discovered them for weeks. The village winds down to this beach and the street ends in a stone wall above the sand. Two little shops serve ice cream and teas, and a rickety wooden jetty makes it possible for sailing dinghies to be tied up while their weary owners recuperate their strength at the pub further up the village. I wonder what are the hazards of being drunk in charge of a sailboat? The jetty also enables a few small motorized fishing boats to organize their lobster potting and offer trips up the river when the tide's right. Quite a lot of people occupy the beach on a summer day, but this only makes a walk with Joey more interesting as he persistently sniffs at every pair of feet he can find, probably as part of a mission to recover his former owner, and this gives the opportunity to form an endless variety of new relationships.

I used to like taking Sebastian to beaches when we could get away from the city. It was easier when I managed to buy a car, but when he was still small we used to go by train with picnic bag and push chair. When we weren't walking I would sit and read a book and Sebastian would eat sand and shells and fill his welly boots with water which he then tipped into his bucket. I realized that he was experimenting with the conservation of volume and let him get on with it. After all, it only took a week or two to dry them out afterwards.

Mother is asking questions about why we have been here three weeks and not heard from Sebastian. I feel sure she is beginning to suspect the truth but I rather think she would consider it bad manners to bring up the subject directly unless I mention it first. I don't want to discuss it with her at the moment.

BEAD: a small ornament with a hole in it that can be threaded onto a string. Beads are made into necklaces, earrings, bracelets, curtains, bags and can even be sewn together to make dresses or stuck onto anything that needs to be decorated. They can also take on a sacred significance. Both Roman Catholics and Moslems use strings of beads as reminders in prayer and, of course, they are also used to make abacuses, or abaci, as I mentioned earlier. On the whole they seem to be fairly superfluous articles, in spite of their many uses, because everything they do can be done more simply by something else; even the praying bit if you really believe that God counts prayers by quantity rather than quality.

I still have a string of beads left with me by Bruce Wild. Bruce remained a hippy long after the fashion had died out. His long hair and beads and Indian shirts made him stand out among other men of his age, and I admired him for his adherence to his youthful principles when the others had retreated to the compromise of collar length hair, corduroys and Marks & Spencer shirts. It took me a while to realize that Bruce was very adept at using to his advantage the attention that his rather attractive and unusual appearance gained him, and that perhaps adherence to youthful principles wasn't the whole story.

BEAR: to carry or put up with, usually referring to some kind of burden, either real or metaphorical. Also a furry animal, ranging in size from large to enormous, and usually dangerous if disturbed. I have never met a bear except in a zoo.

Pope reminds me of a bear. Not only because he's round and hairy but because he ambles into situations without any appreciation of the disturbance and destruction that might be caused by his presence. Take

34

his relationship with Sebastian, for instance. I didn't hesitate long over this because I thought it might be a good thing for Sebastian, who had occasionally asked about his father. I couldn't see any possibility of emotional entanglements arising for me because by then I knew that I had never felt in any way emotional about Pope except in orgasm. I had felt only relief when we parted. But I was concerned enough to insist that Pope should not be immediately introduced as Sebastian's father. I suggested that the introduction should be made tactfully and by degrees but Pope was against this. 'He'll resent it if he thinks we've deceived him.'

'He might resent it even more if he thinks you expect him to accept you without question. Better to get to know each other first.' I knew, and Pope didn't, just how withdrawn and unpredictable Sebastian could be. I couldn't really tell Pope that I was trying to protect him as much as Sebastian. It didn't seem to cross his mind that they might not like each other or that Sebastian had a right to reject the relationship if he didn't find it congenial. Finally I extracted a promise from Pope that he would do things my way, and so one evening he gave me a lift home from the Uni and came in for a drink. Sebastian was already at home, in front of the television, making one of those ghastly constructions they invent on *Blue Peter* with the purpose, it always seems to me, of driving parents beyond endurance. I wonder how many children have been attacked by their mothers as a direct result of *Blue Peter*'s bright ideas? Surrounded by layers of newspaper, glue, string, scissors, silver foil and cornflakes boxes, the contents of which I later discovered had been tipped into a mixing bowl in the kitchen, Sebastian had little time for either of us. I quickly checked that he wasn't actually cutting up the carpet, then brought in two glasses of sherry and Pope sat down on the disintegrating settee and watched his son intently. Sebastian kept his eyes on Peter Purves. The end product of all the effort seemed to be some kind of giant space suit.

Pope took off his glasses and polished them with a hanky, put them on again and still stared at Sebastian. Finally he said to me in a husky voice, 'Are you *sure* about this?'

I knew what he meant and I felt rattled. 'No possible room for doubt.'

'But how do women work these things out?'

'I could only get pregnant by someone I was sleeping with.'

'You mean I was the only one?'

'What did you think?' My head buzzed with mingling anger and disbelief. Did he really mean this?

He gave a boyish and apologetic smile. 'Well, that middle-European sociology tutor was very interested in you and he hinted plainly to our group that he was having if off with you. We all thought that was how you got your high grades.'

Sebastian looked up. 'Could you please keep your voices down?' he asked politely.

I was too frozen to speak and Pope obviously realized he had been impolitic. After another long silent stare at Sebastian he said, 'I had hoped he might be a little more . . . attractive . . . you know . . .'

'How was that possible?'

He looked at me closely and nodded. 'Yes, I see what you mean.'

I rather thought he didn't. I looked from Sebastian's straggly figure to Pope's round one—each seemed to be expanding in a different direction—and I had to admit that for the two greatest things that had ever happened to me they were a pretty disappointing pair.

Sebastian looked up again. 'If you two are going to have a row could you go into the kitchen?' he asked.

'I don't believe it,' hissed Pope.

'It's called autonomy. Do you want to stay for supper?'

BEAT: to hit something or someone, or to overcome. For a moment I thought I would have to include another definition, for the beat of music, but of course this comes from musicians keeping time by hitting something to tap out a regular rhythm. Similarly with the use of 'beat' when we mean we're tired. When I say I'm dead beat I mean I'm beaten, or overcome by tiredness. This happens to me fairly frequently.

BEAUTY: physical or spiritual loveliness, in accordance with a pre-conceived social image of perfection. Mother measured up well on this when she was young—they even photographed her once and put her on a chocolate box and I believe Father almost broke off their engagement when he found out. Kate would be beautiful by anyone's standards if she didn't look so tired out, but I don't believe Kate has had more than four hours' sleep a night for the past ten years, between Andy and the children. I have my health but I don't look at myself in a mirror often enough to be concerned about my face. My photographs frighten or embarrass me and I vaguely feel that's the effect my face must have on the people who look at it, until they get used to it. Mother says I don't make enough effort. She says look at Julia, how much she makes of herself. It is difficult not to look at Julia, she's so stunning, but Julia has time, and incentive; I mean, she *wants* men to drool over her.

BECKON: a gesture of the finger, commanding someone to come towards you. Usually used by policemen or headmasters, or lovers trying in a playful way to establish their dominance.

BED: a piece of furniture for resting or sleeping on. Also of course, in most people's minds, for making love. Whether it's sleep or sex that's most important for you, bed can be an adventure, a comfort or a torment. I like to think of my bed as a private place where I can withdraw from the world at the end of the day and with a bit of luck enter into the most amazing dreams. This doesn't mean that I don't know about the joys of the close intimate sleep that comes to lovers. I do, but to be realistic one night is enough. Six months with Pope was too much. He snored and threshed about and deprived me of my share of the covers. I did try it again later but none of the pleasure quite made up for a heavy head on my shoulder, a growing beard scraping against my neck and pins and needles in my arms. As far as I'm concerned sex and sleep do not mix well. Many people think this is an odd point of view.

BEE: a small flying insect that gathers pollen and makes honey. It was a bee that made my first Cornish cricket match so memorable.

I've never felt any real involvement in cricket at any level. It's not that the intricacies of the game escape me; I'm quite well aware of most of its finer points and I even used to watch Sebastian playing for his school, in the days before he denounced team games as lightly disguised attempts to foster nationalism and refused to take part. I understand the game, I just don't enjoy it. I think this may have something to do with an underlying resentment about never having been allowed to play it. But last week it was almost impossible to avoid involvement. Nancy baked and Mother packed a basket with cakes for the visitors' tea. Joan worried about the weather all day Friday and most of Thursday. Rog and Melly practised, mostly in an adjoining field, and the Commander whistled loudly as he whitened two pairs of boots. When Saturday afternoon came I was drawn in the vortex towards the village green.

The bee? Oh yes, it settled in the flowers in Mother's hat while Mother was sitting innocently in the sun on a deckchair, doing her embroidery and chatting to the Rector who was waiting his turn to go in. It was becoming a long wait because Gabby was accumulating runs with effortless grace. This so infuriated the visiting team that a rather nasty atmosphere was developing, especially since she had been largely responsible for bowling most of them out for a total of forty-eight runs. I had quite enjoyed this spectacle because, while sitting on the pavilion steps, I had heard sniggers and suggestive asides about where she might want to wear her box.

Anyway, Gabby had just hit another four which trickled neatly through a very obvious gap in the outfield when the bee, becoming a trifle frustrated at finding no pollen, moved from a plastic daisy to a plastic freesia, with a buzz loud enough to attract the Rector's attention. He cried, 'Oh I say, hold on!' and swatted Mother neatly on the head with his batting gloves. Mother screamed and clutched her hat and the deckchair collapsed. Everyone around was gripped with an overpowering combination of hysteria and concern and amid the hubbub twenty pairs of arms tried to right Mother while the Rector hopped from one foot to the other, aghast at what he had done. Gabby's attention was diverted just as the ball left the bowler's hand and her wicket was demolished. No one noticed this except the bowler and Gabby, as all the other players had swung round in alarm and, with hands shading their eyes, stood gazing towards the pavilion in bewilderment, and thus missed their moment of triumph.

Apologies were made and Mother restored herself with commendable grace, but for the rest of the summer nobody ever thought of that afternoon without a giggle. Mother never wore the hat again. On the day when I was packing to leave the cottage I found Joan clutching it and wiping tears of silent laughter from her eyes. I gave it to her as a keepsake and in the Rector's Christmas card was a note saying that it now hangs in the pavilion bar in a place of honour beside the Cornish Villages League Shield.

4   Cabbage—Chant

CABBAGE: a large green vegetable, full of vitamins, tasty
and easy to grow. I suppose eating cabbage isn't everyone's idea of a treat but after I'd found out how that red
food dye damages brain cells I began to read some
research papers about food additives. I frightened
myself so much that before long Sebastian and I were
living entirely on wholefood and some home-grown vegetables. Of course it wasn't possible to stick to that
entirely, but by digging up the flower-beds in our tiny
garden and planting cabbages and runner beans we did
pretty well. Sebastian, aged nine, was very interested in
growing things but unfortunately he was also enthusiastic for experiment. After he got the hang of the way
nature had arranged things he would gather seeds and
cuttings from far and wide. The oddest plants would
flourish in cherished nooks and crannies and I could no
longer comfortably discard anything as a weed.

CAGE: an enclosure for keeping animals in, sometimes
people I suppose.
   A small cage appeared in the garden of the cottage
with two guinea-pigs in it. Its advent seems to have
something to do with the Commander; he fusses around
back and forth through the door in the wall. When he
isn't on our side the children and Joey are on the other
side. He's taken them all out sailing in his little dinghy
which seems to me to be a highly risky procedure. I
mean, he must have commanded something rather

larger by way of vessels and have had something more reliable by way of crew. But they all came back safely. Gabby didn't go with them. She often isn't at home.

I worry about the guinea-pigs. When he's not out with the children Joey sits in front of their cage, mouth watering.

CALCULATE: to work out something by using mathematics, or to plan ahead for a particular purpose.

I have to admit that Pope was probably calculating when he invited me to interview for the job. He must have known who I was from the moment he looked at my application form and my qualifications can't have been any more outstanding than those of dozens of other applicants. I do know, though, that I was the best candidate at the interview. I was the only one who had any idea about work in the field; the others were academics full of book theories. I think that if I hadn't been any good Pope couldn't have pushed my appointment past the rest of the panel, but even if I hadn't got the job he could have asked to see Sebastian. It might have been an impulse, but I think he was still calculating after supper when I'd put Sebastian to bed. He put an arm round my waist, clumsily pulled me towards him and nibbled my ear. I found him quite resistible.

'I don't really go in for that sort of thing any more,' I told him.

'In general, or me in particular?'

'In general,' I lied. I had to take account of the fact that he was my boss with my future career in his hands, and it was very nearly true, anyway until Bruce came to work with us the following term.

He turned his back on me with a shrug. 'I'm not surprised really. You always were a cold person.'

My indifference stirred into dislike. 'It depends on the temperature of the water. I really think we ought to try to get on with each other and reviving our physical relationship isn't going to help that.'

He raised his hands in condescending mock surrender. 'You're right, of course. May I take Sebastian to the zoo on Saturday?'

'I wanted to go to Mother's this weekend. What about the following Saturday?'

'Can't manage that. I'm getting married then.'

CAMP: an outdoor settlement, usually temporary.

When the heatwave began Rog and Melly wanted to make camp in the garden. Joan found some old sheets and tablecloths and the Commander encouraged them to hijack the clothes line and showed them how to make a tent between two of the apple trees beyond the vegetable garden. An expedition set off for Truro to buy waterproof sleeping bags and a new clothes line, and the children moved out of the cottage.

CANNABIS: a plant which acts as an intoxicant, argued to be harmless but I have other beliefs about that. At first I didn't recognize it growing in a corner of the garden and when Bruce told me what it was I said, 'Oh Lord, Sebastian's overdone it this time,' and pulled it up and threw it on the rubbish heap. I expected Sebastian to be upset, as he'd always been in the past when I'd interfered with his gardening experiments, but he just came in the next day rather tight-lipped and got on with his homework, an unusual occurrence in itself. I ought to have been warned. A few months later I found the same plant growing again, this time on the edge of the rubbish heap and I thought a few seeds had been accidentally dropped from the old plant.

CANTANKEROUS: bad tempered.

Bassett is a cantankerous man. He is the aged gardener Mother engaged. He is very thin and bent, as though suffering from permanent stomach ache or contraction of the chest muscles. Either condition must be painful enough to account for his bad temper. His only form of communication appears to be complaints about cricket on the lawn, dogs on the flower-beds, rain not falling, and people picking the vegetables before they're ready. Nancy said not to take any notice, he didn't really mean any of it, but he had to be taken seriously the day the camp fire was lit in the orchard. Mother was out at the time helping the Rector's wife to make pincushions for the cricket club fête. I was the only responsible representative of the household. He intercepted me in front of the cottage just as I was setting off for an afternoon walk.

'It's them or me!' he raged. 'Them or me!'

I caught the gist of his argument immediately. 'Well, we do *have* to keep them.' I explained. We didn't want to lose him but I could see no alternative. 'Couldn't you possibly overlook whatever it is this time?'

'But they've lit a fire! 'Tis tinder dry out there. If it catches it'll spread to your thatch. You'll not overlook it then!'

'I'll explain that to them.'

'And what about the alyssum? Will you explain that too?'

'What about the alyssum?'

'It keeps getting eaten. Will you explain that too?'

'The children eat the alyssum?' Those little white flowers around the edge of the lawn? Surely not.

He looked at me as though I was a bigger fool than he'd imagined. 'No, not the children! That darn tortoise!'

'Tortoise? Have we got a tortoise?'

'Them kids have, and it's mighty fond of alyssum. Can you get it under control before it finds the lettuce?'

'I doubt it.' Uncontrollable tortoises were not part of my experience.

Bassett did stay on because the children were persuaded that they could survive on food from the kitchen instead of cooking their own. The tortoise had a piece of string tied around one leg and was tethered to a stake in the middle of the lawn. There he was fed on the outside

43

leaves of lettuces from the kitchen. He sulked for several days and then escaped. He hasn't actually been seen since but nearly all the alyssum around the lawn has disappeared by now.

CARE: to look after a person or thing.

Caring is an unpredictable business. I wonder which of my students will survive as caring people and which will be hardened and chewed up after five years of other people's problems. At a departmental meeting Pope voiced the view that we weren't doing enough to develop the caring instinct in our students. He introduced us to the caring egg idea. This was thought up in some university on the other side of the Atlantic to awaken the awareness of caring in social work students. Each student is given an egg which has to be carefully looked after for a whole week. The egg mustn't be out of the student's sight for all that time; must be beside him as he sleeps; must accompany him everywhere. A daily report has to be written on the way the relationship with the egg is developing.

As a department of serious educators we took it pretty well, though the stunned silence after Pope had finished explaining this idea was a bit of a giveaway. Then Pope lifted his briefcase onto the table and took out, very gently, a dozen fresh eggs. 'Before we ask our students to do anything we're going to try it ourselves. For a week, ladies and gentlemen, we are going to become egg carers.' Was he serious? A little ripple of doubt passed through the group, then the eggs were handed out and Pope took one for himself. 'Now remember, complete honesty, with yourselves as well as with one another. In one week's time we'll meet again and share our experiences.'

For the next couple of days we laughed about it but then it became noticeable that there were little bulges in people's pockets and in quiet moments hands would slip into the warmth and close around the precious objects.

Pope ostentatiously carried his in his hand everywhere and set it down carefully beside him whenever he needed both hands. After the third day the eggs weren't mentioned at all but an atmosphere of furtive mistrust began to creep into departmental relationships. One senior lecturer was found in an empty staff room talking quietly to himself with his egg on his lap.

What did I do? I took mine home after that first meeting and put it down on the kitchen table, meaning to come to some understanding with it later. Then I became involved in housework and went down the road to the launderette. When I got back Sebastian had decided to make his own tea and was happily boiling *my* egg!

'My God, Sebastian, that's my egg you're boiling!'

'Hey, Mum, there's plenty more in the cupboard.'

'But that's the egg I'm supposed to look after!' I picked up a spoon and fished it out of the water, examining it carefully for cracks. Sebastian shook his head. 'Jesus, Mum, you really are a nut!' he muttered as he fetched another egg out of the box in the cupboard. I was concerned about Sebastian's assessment of me. I could see that it would affect his stability to feel that his only parent was losing a grip on reality. But I was also thinking about the egg. I had two alternatives: either to continue to care for a boiled version, which after all had the advantage that it wouldn't come to harm so easily, or to substitute a replacement, and I couldn't be sure that Pope hadn't marked the eggs in some subtle way. At that point it never occurred to me to return eggless at the end of the week and admit that I had left my precious charge untended for long enough for disaster to befall.

So I popped it back into the water to finish boiling and asked Sebastian not to tell Pope about this.

He nodded and muttered, 'Another nut.' Then after a moment's consideration he said, 'I know I shouldn't interfere in your choice of boyfriends but he really gives me the creeps.'

'You have every right to express an opinion.' I had

always stuck to this principle even though I hadn't always liked the opinions I had heard. 'But Pope isn't my boyfriend. Just an old friend whom I work with now.'

'Thank goodness for that. I thought he might be moving in or something. I really can't take the funny way he looks at me.'

By that time I was sleeping with Bruce, but discreetly, because it was only for sex and I didn't want the hassle of drawing him into my private life with Sebastian. Pope came in for coffee occasionally and tried selfconsciously to strike up conversations with Sebastian and to complain to me about the furnishings his wife had chosen for their house. I knew that I was soon going to have to break the truth to Sebastian but it isn't easy to decide how a thirteen-year-old boy will take news like that so I put it off.

I carried a hard-boiled egg around with me, almost feeling smug, and wrote a daily report about our activities, and I felt a great sense of relief that nothing I could do to it would damage it. At the meeting the following week we all came in and set down our eggs, with suspicious glances around the table and none of the pleasant social chat that usually marked our conversation on these occasions. I noticed that one or two people had unaccustomed dark rings under their eyes. Pope came in last and set down his egg, then asked us if we would like to take it in turns to summarize our relationships with our charges. Bruce, whom I hadn't seen all week, explained seriously how constrained he had felt and how the presence of the egg had begun to inhibit all his normal social responses. He said he was grateful to Pope for the experiment which had showed him exactly what a relationship with a child would do to him, and had decided him never to become a father.

'But that's not a fair trial!' exclaimed the other woman in the department, who was hopelessly in love with Bruce. 'You've been experiencing a one-way relationship. The egg hasn't responded as a child would.'

46

Bruce fixed her with a beady eye. 'Are you trying to suggest that my egg hasn't been responsive?'

She clucked and swallowed, her physical responses as usual reduced to chaos by Bruce's attention. I was glad that he didn't do that to me.

Pope turned to the next person, an earnest young man who, like me, was a junior lecturer. 'What about you, Andrew? How do you feel about your egg?'

Andrew picked it up and held it in the palm of his hand. He was trembling. With a slow movement he closed his fingers around the egg and shattered the shell. A unified gasp came from all around the table. Yolk and albumen dripped from his fist onto the table. Tears streamed down his face and I couldn't decide whether they were tears of grief or laughter.

It was my turn next and I had abandoned all my plans to pander to Pope's seriousness. I was going to eat my egg in front of them all as an act of defiance. But I didn't get a chance. Suddenly a strange scratching sound diverted our attention to Pope's briefcase on the floor beside him. He picked it up and looked inside and his face was a mixture of several very strong emotions. Then he turned puce and stormed out of the room. It was Bruce who put a hand into the briefcase and drew out a very dishevelled and angry chick. We never discovered who had put it there.

CAT: a smallish, furry mammal, domesticated. There are the large and wild varieties, of course, but fortunately restricted to zoos and films in my experience. I bought Sebastian a kitten for his sixth birthday and one day I found him trying to teach it to swim in the bath. Having little choice in the matter, other than drowning, the cat actually did negotiate the length of the bath before I was attracted by the fearful noise and rescued it. The cat not only survived but formed an amazing attachment for Sebastian above all other humans. It would sit on the window-sill and look out for his return from school, sit beside his bed if he was ill, and refuse food put down by anyone but him. In the end it even came on holiday with us. As it grew older it began to go blind, and when Sebastian wasn't around it spent most of the time on his bed, except for necessary sorties into the garden. A week after Sebastian's disappearance it was run over in the street.

CAVE: an opening in rocks, leading underground. There are quite a few along our stretch of beach, as the coastline develops into a headland. The cliff becomes steep and rugged and the sea has worn away several caves that are quite deep and join up with each other in such a way as to set the children off playing interesting games of ambush. Further up the face of the cliff there are other caves that might well join with the lower ones but investigation of the matter seems unnecessarily risky. Rog and Melly were all for undertaking this project and I forbade them ever to try, though without a great deal of faith that they would obey me if it came to the point.

'Gabby's been up there,' Melly complained as we walked back along the beach. Well, bully for Gabby. 'We saw her, you know, coming out of one, yesterday afternoon. She came down a little broken path. She was so surprised to find us waiting at the bottom.'

'What was she doing there?'

'Looking for smugglers,' Rog said, giving Melly such a secret and angry look that I wondered if they'd been asked not to tell anyone about it.

'And did she find one?'

'Don't be silly, there aren't any smugglers now.'

'But she says there used to be smugglers using the caves and one stormy night some men were hiding in there and part of the cliff fell down and buried them for ever.'

'Well doesn't that just go to show that I'm right about it being dangerous up there!' I exclaimed thankfully. They don't often play into my hands.

'That was a stormy night. Surely we can go up on a fine afternoon?'

Apart from accidents I was a trifle concerned about what they might find up there. The smugglers might not be the only people with secrets to hide. 'Listen, if either of you two goes up there and I find out about it, which I almost certainly will, I'll send you back to your father and he can do what he likes with you until your mother's better.'

'Please! Please!' screamed Melly, almost doubling up with laughter. 'Please don't do that! He'll lock us in the airing-cupboard and sell us to slave traders! Oh mercy! Have mercy!'

But Roger stuffed his hands into his pockets and scowled, kicking at a bit of seaweed. 'I like it here,' he said, 'but when's Mum going to be better?'

'You had a postcard from her this morning. She's out of hospital but resting at home.'

'Who's looking after her?'

'A home help comes every day and Daddy's with her in the evenings.'

Roger looked even more worried. 'He won't like that.'

In fact his worries were soon brought to an end because the following weekend, without warning, Andy appeared in his large new car with Kate and the other three children. Kate was pale and exhausted and the baby was crying. Stevie and Miranda were hot and bad tempered.

'How lovely to see you,' Mother exclaimed as they piled out of the car. 'But just a teeny bit of notice would have made all the difference.'

'But didn't you get my postcard?' I caught Andy's eye as he said this and I'm sure he blushed under his already pink complexion. Andy never writes, only phones. He'd been scared that we wouldn't let them all come. Mother knew this too but she said, 'Oh dear, one really can't rely on the post nowadays.' Mother has a far more forgiving nature than I shall ever be able to cultivate. 'You'd better all come in. Sally, I think we'll put Kate and the baby in the housekeeper's flat in the extension. You take Stevie and the baby and show her the way and the other children can help Andy unpack the luggage.'

She disappeared into the house unencumbered and I heard her busy on the telephone. She quickly came to a generous financial arrangement with Joan's eldest daughter who had just left school and wanted to be a nursery nurse. Within two hours Joan and young Jennifer had swooped on us, made beds, fed children, unpacked suitcases and borrowed the car so that Jennifer's belongings could be moved in too. I chased out the children and Joey and put Kate to bed for a rest. 'Whose is that dog?' she asked me weakly as they all hurtled past the window.

'Yours.'

She shook her head. 'No, I don't think so.' I wondered who was going to win that one.

Outside I found Andy sitting on the hammock, well fed, sipping beer from a pint mug. He was surveying the garden with dazed relief. He didn't even ask where everyone was. He jumped as I came towards him and I almost began to feel sorry for him for having been landed with more than he'd ever bargained for.

'I suppose you're not staying?'

'I really can't,' he said happily. 'Much as I would like to join your peaceful little establishment. I have to catch a plane to Brussels early tomorrow morning. The European conference, you know. Must set off home this evening.'

'Kate doesn't look too well.'

'No, she hasn't been pulling round the way she should. That's why I brought her down. The doctor says she needs complete rest, and she just won't get it at home. Keeps feeling she has to do little things even though I tell her I can manage perfectly well. It's such a relief to know she'll be in good hands now.'

I wondered if he really did have to go to Brussels but I

50

decided to concede the point and let him off with good grace. His nerves were obviously shot to pieces. As we talked there came a savage scream from the direction of the raspberry canes, followed by excited barking from Joey. Andy jumped and turned pale and sweat stood out on his brow. 'My God, what's that?'

'Only a dog.'

'No, the other?'

'Well it might be the Commander playing Red Indians or it might be the gardener murdering one of the children.'

Just then the box hedge parted in an unlikely place and Miranda, the eldest child, came rushing across the lawn waving her arms. 'Daddy! Daddy! There's a tent in the garden where Rog and Melly live and it's got a real live Indian squaw in it!'

Squaw? Gabby?

'They *live* there?' gasped Andy.

'They sleep out on fine nights and have picnics and things,' I explained, but got no further because Andy's attention was rivetted on Gabby striding across the lawn wearing a white fringed bikini with her hair loosely plaited into two long black ropes.

'Hello there, Sally. Fancy you not being locked up with your work. The old man's playing golf so I thought I'd pop in for a drink. Whose amazing car is that in the drive?'

Andy leaped up, beaming. 'It's mine. Do you like it? In a bit of a mess now, after the drive down, but I'll give you a closer look if you like.'

She fixed her large eyes on Andy as though he was a god. 'Oh yes, please.' Andy took her arm and steered her round the corner of the house. Before they disappeared she called back, 'Gin and tonic please, Sally.'

As the engine roared and the tyres scrunched on the drive, Miranda ran back to her brother and sister calling, 'Hey! Daddy's taken the squaw for a ride!' I wondered how it had escaped me that Gabby was a car

51

enthusiast. I knew she liked cricket and gardens and caves but the car angle was new. I poured her gin and tonic and left it in the sun, hoping the ice would melt before they came back.

CEMENT: a grey powdery substance which, when mixed with water, hardens and binds together bricks, stones and anything else that becomes involved. For most mixing purposes it has to be diluted with sand, or with chippings if a rough surface is needed, and this mixture is known as concrete. The proportions of the mix are very important to the setting time and final durability of the work. Sometimes people get this wrong and then buildings collapse.

This information came to me via Miranda and Rog and Melly, who gleaned it from Bassett while he was mixing concrete to repair the crazy paving path. They had been strictly forbidden to go anywhere near the job, for obvious reasons, so they compromised by sitting at a safe distance and asking questions, thereby infuriating Bassett while not actually interfering with his work. It was during the progress of this that the tortoise came back into our lives and sadly out of his. During the lunch break a bucket of wet concrete was left on a step against a wall overhung with alyssum. The tortoise, in his relentless hunt for his favourite food, was having to get into more and more difficult places to find it and had obviously been driven to walk along the top of the wall. He fell into the bucket of concrete and panicked. I believe that if he'd kept perfectly still the density of the concrete would have supported him, but he couldn't be expected to know this and he struggled to free himself and so became quite firmly embedded. By the time Bassett came back from his lunch all that was showing was his shell.

There was much grief and also a certain amount of ill feeling because Roger suspected that Bassett had spotted the tortoise on the wall and had purposely placed the bucket in a strategic position. Kate, lying in the hammock on the verandah, sipping a coffee, sympathized gently, but I could see she was secretly relieved. She regarded the menagerie of animals as an affront to her authority. In her view they were destructive and unhygienic, and she had never allowed the children to keep pets at home. The fewer there were to bid farewell to at the end of the summer, the happier their departure would be.

After an hour spent crouched in the middle of the lawn wailing over the corpse, from which all traces of concrete had been carefully washed, a decision was made. Mother and I had joined Kate on the verandah and watched the scene with unease. We were relieved when the wailing stopped and conversation began, then Melly picked up the corpse and they set off in procession, followed by Stevie and Jennifer.

'Are they going to bury it?' Mother called to Jennifer.

She shook her head and came running back. 'They're taking it to Potty Peter.'

'Potty Peter?'

'You know, Peter Potter, that fisherman who makes the shell souvenirs and stuffs the seagulls. He'll know what to do about it.

'Shell souvenir or stuffed tortoise?' I asked. I assumed they didn't expect him to bring the creature back to life.

'That's what we want advice about.'

'In that case I think Stevie should stay here.' Kate saw danger everywhere outside the garden.

Jennifer's face clouded. It was her responsibility to look after Stevie and if he stayed then she had to. She had become as caught up in the tortoise preservation project as the children: well, she was a child too, really. But she seized hold of Stevie and turned back. I went upstairs to my workroom to claim what was left of the afternoon and didn't enquire whether she managed to keep him imprisoned or not.

*   *   *

CHAD: a large but very shallow lake in Central Africa. In the rainy season it almost trebles its size and water birds build nests and lay eggs along its shore. When the waters dry up the birds depart in a flock and any young birds that are still unable to fly are left to die of thirst and starvation. I wonder if the mother birds care, or even notice?

CHALLENGE: a difficult or testing problem to overcome. My life seems to be full of these. No sooner have I overcome one challenge than another arises. I have sometimes suspected that this is a case of divine punishment for ignoring society's conventions over the marriage situation. Some of my problems can be accounted for without bringing God into it but other things are really not my fault. As soon as I get one area of my life organized disaster strikes elsewhere. Mother says it's because of my attitude. Some people, she says, sit and watch the world go by while others stick out their necks and give it a push every now and again. I think this comment is extremely unfair.

CHANT: a simple tune, or a continuously repeated slogan uttered in a singsong voice.
All the adults soon learned to recognize the chanting in the garden as a sign of some new project afoot. It would start up somewhere in the undergrowth, always accompanied by a background of barking, come nearer and nearer, pass along the paths of the vegetable garden, behind the box hedge, along the drive. Sometimes it would be diverted through the gate into the Commander's garden, sometimes it would trail away down the lane towards the beach. Strangely, there was seldom any visible evidence of the cause of the noise. Kate would usually stop what she was doing and listen carefully, for it was the only contact she had with her three eldest children. They had ceased to appear at mealtimes. If enquiries were made Nancy replied that they had

taken off a pile of sandwiches or a pie and as she seemed able to cope with this no one worried further. I made an assumption, without foundation it was true, that someone saw to baths and clean clothes from time to time, and made sure they went to bed at night. It later transpired that everyone had been making the same assumption about some member of the household and in fact the children had more or less ceased to have any contact at all with the adult world.

I have now managed to complete two chapters of my thesis which is a little behind schedule. I know I'm always too optimistic about my schedules anyway, but Kate needs company and while the weather is so hot it's very hard to stay cooped up indoors for more than half a day. If God was on my side it would rain all the time and my room would be a cosy haven. You see what I mean about divine retribution? It happens all the time.

5   Dead—Date

DEAD: this is the first word I think of in the Ds and all I
see in my mind are the pictures of drug addicts and
junkies dying in filthy lavatories and tatty bedsitters,
unable to help themselves and unhelped by the people
who could be/should be loving them. Is this Sebastian?
Where did he/why did he go like that? If I scrabble in
my purse I can find his note, but I don't need to, I know it
by heart. 'Drown but not out, flighting back, stay
turned.' Now is that the last cry of a sinking person or a
burst of optimism?

DABBLE: this should really come first in this section if the
previous world hadn't crept in by unfair means. To dabble is to dip in here and there, really into water, but it
has come to be understood as dipping into many affairs,
though none very deeply. A dabbler is a person who
knows a little about a lot of things, who is always
engaged in some different project.
    The best example of a dabbler I have at present is
Peter Potter. The children were delighted when they
collected their tortoise from him, some days after the
Dreadful Incident. He was varnished and lively looking,
just stepping out, head erect and inquisitive, with a
knowing smile on his little lacquered face that seemed,
impossibly, to be reflected in his bead eyes. He looked
far more intelligent now than he had alive, though when
I consider that he had actually shown quite a lot of cun-
ning in dealing with his situation, until his last escapade,

perhaps he had always looked intelligent and I just hadn't noticed. Anyway, Peter Potter was clearly a skilled preserver of tortoises.

'Does he want paying?' Kate asked, bravely examining the handiwork.

'We asked him that,' Miranda said, 'and he said no.'

'He didn't,' Melly contradicted. 'He said, "Not a bit of it, my lovers. A favour given is a favour gained." '

'And what sort of favour does he want from you?' wondered Kate.

They did look a bit puzzled at this. 'Nothing so far. But he did say we could go for a ride in his boat for nothing when he didn't have a full load of passengers.'

'Not quite free,' Rog reminded them. 'He wants us to help with collecting the money and winding up the ropes and things.'

'Oh yes, but that's nothing!'

'I absolutely forbid it!' Kate said, but fortunately for her authority her words were drowned by a diversion as the guinea-pigs escaped and had to be rescued from Joey.

It seemed that Peter had a ramshackle cruiser large enough to take passengers around the headland, out on deep-sea fishing trips, and across the channel. Joan told us this after an enquiry from Mother, who was certainly more diplomatic about these things than Kate. It was hinted that Peter brought back things he oughtn't to from his trips abroad.

'Drugs?' asked Mother, while Kate shuddered slightly.

'Oh no, nothing like that. Mostly wine and brandy, we think.'

'Really? And what happens to it?'

'Well, there's those who say that he drinks it himself, and I must say he does seem to try sometimes. But we have noticed, my brother and I, that there are often some very unusually labelled bottles of French wines on the shelf of the village shop.'

This shop was no longer a cosy, brown-varnished,

old-fashioned emporium, but a streamlined minimarket with post office and off-licence attached. I reflected that the Rector and his sister must really know their wines to be able to detect smuggled brands. I wondered if they bought them, and at what cut price. As this thought crossed my mind, Joan blushed and continued. 'He's very good with his hands, old Potter. You know, he makes all those souvenirs he sells in that little shop of his. Spends all the winter doing them.'

'The children seem very attached to him.'

'Well, I don't know, I don't want to meddle, but do you think, I mean, he's a very *engaging* character, there's no doubt of that, but, well, not quite, you know, *nice* for little children to be around with.'

'Not nice?' She made it sound like rude words in school.

'Well, there's other things . . .'

'Such as?'

'I wouldn't like to say.' And she didn't.

'They'll have to be stopped,' Kate said firmly, meaning the children.

'We've all tried to stop them, in a roundabout way, but they don't seem to care about public opinion.'

'Joan dear,' Mother insisted, 'would you say that the children are in any sort of danger from this man?'

'Not actual danger in itself, just that they might hear things, you know . . .'

I wasn't at all sure that Mother did know because I certainly didn't, and when Kate said again that the children had to be kept away from him I asked her how she thought she was going to do it.

'I'll phone Andy. He'll know what to do. I'll phone him tonight.'

Mother and I both privately decided on two alternative courses of action. I made up my mind to go and seek out Potter, reasoning that I was qualified to make some sort of judgement about him. Mother took herself off to the Forresters and grilled the Commander. She came back several gin and tonics later full of reassurance.

'There's nothing to worry about. The man's quite harmless really. Likes his drink and likes the women, but he's not a child molester.'

Kate couldn't get through to Andy and when he did eventually phone her from Paris he said he was sure that Mother and Sally could deal with the situation. If he'd said it to me I'd have reminded him whose children they were but Kate said, 'Of course,' and spent the whole of the next day in a deep depression wondering if Andy really needed to go to Paris to sell lawnmowers.

DACOIT: a bandit, of Eastern origin, who sneaks up in the dark and murders his victims before robbing them. You may think that this nasty kind of activity only happens in far-flung places but it seems to be very like that of the Cornish Wreckers who used to lure ships onto the rocks by showing lights that misled the sailors into thinking they were coming into port. Those seamen and passengers who managed to swim ashore were hacked to pieces by the Wreckers and their clothes and jewellery stolen from their bodies. When I think that many of the ancestors of the people who now pass their lives in this village may have been engaged in that grim trade, it seems unjust to shudder at stories of dacoity and be thankful that it's something slippery and foreign.

DAFFODIL: a yellow, frilly flower, the ambassador of spring to many people who see its early arrival in fruit-and-veg shops and therefore do not realize that it is by no means the earliest or the most beautiful of the spring flowers. Also the national flower of Wales but as I don't know any Welsh people and have only visited the place once, to take a summer school course at Bangor University, that side of its fame holds little interest for me. However, it does remind me of Bruce Wild at the time when he became quite inextricably entangled in my life by teaching Sebastian to play football.

There was a large and popular park near to where we lived for many years while Sebastian was growing up. When he was small we spent many happy hours there, playing hide-and-seek among the bushes, paddling silly little boats on the pond, eating ice creams, learning to fly kites and ride bicycles. But by the time he was thirteen or so these pursuits had lost their interest for him. We graduated half-heartedly to crazy golf and some sort of parody of tennis but the truth was that he needed friends of his own age to spend his weekend afternoons with, not a mother, and so we went to the park less and less often. I wouldn't in any way have minded about Sebastian spending time with his friends instead of with me, though I might have worried a bit about what they were getting up to, but he just didn't seem to have the friends hanging around him much. The occasional child would loom on the horizon of our lives, spend a couple of afternoons with Sebastian, or invite him home, and then would be heard of no more. I don't know what he did to them and I didn't press the matter because that would have seemed like interfering.

Anyway, this sunny daffodil day Sebastian did consent to take a stroll in the park and he even rowed me up and down the large lake in an adult-sized rowing boat. It was a rather unnerving experience because of Sebastian's lack of co-ordination which made it unlikely that both the oars would be in the water at the same time, but we made some sort of progress and had just disembarked and bought ice creams when I saw Bruce loping towards us across the grass, looking for all the world like a daffodil himself, his golden hair flowing and gleaming in the sun which also glinted off his wire rimmed spectacles. A bright yellow shirt flapped in the breeze and, to press the point home, a daffodil was perched behind his ear; pinched, no doubt, from one of the flower-beds. He was carrying a sort of net bag in which was a football, but that was black and white, not yellow.

I was a bit surprised because I never saw Bruce

except during the week, as I've already explained, and I knew he didn't live anywhere nearby. But he was obviously making straight for us, as though he'd been expecting to see us. It was no accident. He put an arm around my waist and kissed me on the cheek, which he never normally did anyway and which embarrassed me considerably in front of Sebastian who was looking more interested than I'd seen him for many a month.

I muttered, 'Hello Bruce, what a surprise,' then turned to Sebastian. 'Darling, this is Bruce Wild who works with me at the University.'

'Oh yeah?' said Sebastian unbelievingly and continued to munch his cornet with a knowing look, unmoved by Bruce's friendly greeting. We could do nothing but walk on together while Bruce explained that he had been unable to resist coming to visit us on such a fine spring afternoon, joys of nature, rush of blood etcetera. Not finding us at home he'd thought we might be here, and here we were, and how he'd been looking forward to meeting Sebastian.

'Bruce, why the football?'

'Oh, uh, boys like to play football, don't they?' But he was already aware that he might have seriously misjudged the situation.

'Do they?' queried Sebastian. 'No one told me.'

'Well, I'm pretty good myself. Suppose we give it a try?'

I was surprised that Sebastian agreed but he'd finished his ice cream and there wasn't any other amusement around. Bruce left me in charge of the net bag and set off into the middle distance, dribbling and feinting, followed by Sebastian.

Bruce was quite good, considering his age and occupation, and soon a small group of assorted children gathered and the ensuing game was so disorganized that Sebastian became involved without it mattering that he could hardly kick the ball. But I wasn't content to sit on the sidelines minding the gear and neither did I have any ambition to join in, so I went back to the flat and spent a peaceful hour working on a lecture plan. Then they came back, both soaked to the skin and covered with a sort of green slime. The football had got kicked into the lake and they'd had to hire a boat to fetch it and whilst leaning over to retrieve it Sebastian had tipped them both straight into the water. It had turned out to be shallow but very slimy and muddy and they had waded back, towing the boat behind them.

I suppose I ought to have warned Bruce about Sebastian but it hadn't seemed necessary just for an hour, and anyway Bruce had rather brought it on himself. So I made supper and washed and dried clothes, and Bruce stayed, and that was the beginning of another phase in my life. I knew it had all been set up, except for the dip in the lake, but by some miracle Sebastian actually liked Bruce so I let it happen.

Daffodils—ugh!

DAMAGE: spoiling or breaking something, either deliberately or by accident. I suppose the deliberate damage really goes by the name of Vandalism, from another race of slippery foreigners, but it's the accidental kind that I find most alarming. The trouble is, you can always be sorry you've done damage, after the event, but knowing that it's going to happen is another matter and hard to prevent.

DAMOCLES: I can't leave him out. He was the guy who envied King Dionysus and let it be heard that he thought the king had an easy life. The king didn't see it that way at all so he invited Damocles to a banquet and seated him in a chair which had a sword suspended above it by a single hair, in order to impress upon him how precarious a king's life could be. What a thing to be remembered for; somewhat like Midas and Canute. If I thought my name was going to go down in history I wouldn't want it to be for being caught out in a situation that definitely leaves one looking foolish.

DASH: I can think of three meanings: a dash meaning a short stroke between two words; a dash being a sudden quick journey, as when Mother says, 'I'm just going to dash down to the minimarket'; a dash meaning a small portion, as when Gabby says, 'Just a dash of tonic in that gin!' Three different meanings, all connected by being something swift and short. Then of course there's dashing away with the smoothing iron, which is swift but vigorous, at least the way Nancy does it in the afternoons, helped by the languishing Kate who is now strong enough to fold nappies and towels.

DATE: a numerical label which distinguishes one day from any other in the year and enables one to fix appointments in the future. Also the brown sticky fruit of a particular kind of palm tree. The two are blended together in this fine joke relayed to me from Peter Potter via Miranda: 'What did one palm tree say to the other palm tree?'
  'I don't know, dear. What did . . .?'
  'Let's make a date! Ha! Ha! Ha!'
  I had kept my resolution to seek out Potter and find out what it was about him that was not nice. I found a man rather younger than I'd been led to expect but brown and weathered in a way that made him look wise and aged. His hair and beard were dark and straggly, and as greasy and unwashed as his clothes. I had gone to the little souvenir shop and found Miranda in sole charge, serving some customers. But before long the strange figure of Potter loomed in the doorway, carrying a bucket of fish, accompanied by Roger. 'Hello, my dear,' he boomed. 'You must be Aunt Sally!'
  I shuddered and tried to smile as he continued, 'All right Miranda? How's business?'
  'Splendid. I took ten pounds and sold that quite hideous

pottery cottage. At ten percent that's a pound you owe me.'

'Good girl! Come on Rog, we must get these fish gutted and into the freezer, except your share of course.' They made their way through the shop to the room at the back. Roger's share? What was Roger going to do with fish? Make another camp fire? I jumped up and followed them into the large and untidy living room. 'You've got some fish then, Rog?'

'Yes, look!' He held up two long, floppy bodies. 'We're going to cook them on the beach. It's all right to make a fire on the beach isn't it, Sally?'

'I suppose so. But take care.' Potter was already up to his elbows in a stone sink, scraping and slitting and sloshing nasty things about. He gave me a grin and a wink.

Roger said, 'We'll wait till it's dark and the trippers have gone. Would you like to come along?'

Just then Gabby walked through the door from the shop as though she lived there and no one seemed surprised to see her. But she was surprised to see me and a wave of hostility preceded her smile. 'Hello Sally, you've found the den too, have you?'

Potter's grin was wider still, with an evil glint to it. 'Hello my lady. How're you today?'

It was too late. However casually Gabby moved past him and arranged herself on the corner of the kitchen table there was no mistaking that certain atmosphere or Potter's glances or the suspicion contained in her manner towards me. I knew now what Joan had been trying to say to us, and probably what Gabby did in the caves above the beach.

6   *Debate—Drug*

DEBATE: a rational discussion presenting facts for both sides of a contentious matter. It is essential that those taking part in the debate listen carefully to the facts presented by the opposing interest and take these into account when taking up their theoretical standpoint. Otherwise what is happening is argument, not debate. Many people argue under the impression that they are debating and many people shout in the belief that this gives them a claim to be considered rational.

DECAY: something rotting and crumbling away because of age or lack of repair. Peter Potter's shop-cum-cottage was in this state and was causing problems between him and his landlord, not from the usual angle of the tenant asking for repairs that the landlord is unwilling to pay for, but because the owner wanted to renovate the property and Potter didn't want it touched. Maybe he didn't want to give the owner an excuse to raise the rent but I rather suspect that he had plenty of ready cash. He just don't want his comfortable and unhygienic life style to be imposed upon.

DESOLATE: wretched, lonely and deserted.
I think this is the sort of word Julia would use to describe her state of mind when she turned up to stay with us, except that she seems to have been the one doing the deserting.
I didn't actually see her arrive as I'd gone down to the

beach to join in the fish bonfire. By the time I got there the fire was already alight and the children were spearing slivers of fish on sticks and propping them around the flames. Quite a few actually did get cooked and tasted very good if one didn't mind the occasional crunchy grain of sand.

'Fish and silicon chips,' mused Miranda as we munched.

There's something very alluring about the smell of wood smoke and the deep yellow heart of a fire you've made yourself. As I sat there with these children I was reminded of a time I'd borrowed a tent and taken Sebastian camping in the Lake District. We found a quiet cove and built a fire and actually cooked a complete meal on it. Sebastian collected wood and ate all his food and I could swear he was happy then, though he said little. Later I left the children to enjoy the remainder of the fire, with the typical adult exhortation to be careful and not to be too late, which they treated with the contempt it deserved. Outside the cottage was parked Julia's TR7, gleaming bright yellow in the light from the window, and I found her in the sitting room being comforted in her desolation by Kate and Mother and a very strong whisky. Having just spent two hours on a beach bent over a bonfire and eating smoked fish and sand with my fingers I knew I didn't look my best but I was a bit put out when Julia recoiled and grimaced at the sight of me.

'Sally darling, where *have* you been?' she trilled. There never has been an occasion, even in childhood, when I haven't looked like a scarecrow in comparison with Julia, and she always makes a big thing about it.

'You do smell a bit nasty,' Mother ventured.

'And you're pretty smutty,' offered Kate.

I suppose I must have glowered at them. I had quite enjoyed the little picnic but the children did belong to Kate and this was *my* holiday with Mother. What were they all doing here?

Mother said, 'Julia has just driven all the way from Uppsala. You might show her that you're pleased to see her.'

'Clever Julia! All the way across the North Sea in a TR7? I should think we're lucky to see you!'

'Oh Sally darling, you don't change, do you?' She swept across the room and enclosed me in a delicate embrace which was her usual manner of consoling me for not being beautiful and not having been able to find a rich husband. 'Don't you want to know why I'm here?'

'Let me guess. You're pregnant.' That would be important enough for Julia to want to make the announcement personally.

'Oh God, as though I could be!' She strode the room with a swirl of skirts and a jangle of jewellery. 'Oh no, I've finally come to my senses. I've left that monster Sven!'

Sven had his faults but there was no way he could be described as a monster. I nearly asked whether he had objected to the way Julia spent his money, or tried to stop her sleeping with waiters of Mediterranean origin, but I thought I'd better be kind so I just smiled sweetly and said, 'You poor dear.' I figured that as she'd probably just told Mother and Kate the whole story—well, as much of it as she wanted them to know—she wouldn't want to start again for my benefit just then. I knew I would hear it all before long. I excused myself to have a bath and Mother called after me, 'Don't take all the hot water, Sally. Julia's had a long journey and she needs a soak.'

DETER: to prevent someone from action by making it suit their interests better to be inactive; making the consequences of action seem so frightening that they must be avoided. Unfortunately this doesn't always work out quite so simply.

For instance, Kate was keen on the idea of deterring the children from associating with Peter Potter by threatening to send them home. When it occurred to her that the children would quite certainly see the flaw in this and ask who was going to look after them at home, she threatened to send them to stay with Andy's parents, which did make them think twice because the elder Randolphs were a narrow-minded, bullying couple who lived in an almost inaccessible part of Esher. However, I suspect that this threat only had the effect of making it doubly certain that Kate wouldn't know about anything her children did. As they were already well practised in avoiding detection and laying misleading trails around the village, they were well up to the new challenge. They took the sensible precaution of asking who they were allowed to talk to and, after a lengthy discussion which convinced me that it will be the country's loss if none of them becomes a diplomat, the list of approved people included anyone who was a friend of Joan or Nancy or their children, the people who ran the minimarket, and the Commander and Gabby.

'And their friends?' came the final, clinching question.

'And their friends,' conceded a weary Kate, convinced that she had done a good job.

DIAPHRAGM: a partition which separates two parts of a whole entity.

For instance, it is the band of muscle which separates the lungs and chest organs from the abdominal ones and presumably if it wasn't there the heart, stomach and liver might drift downwards and the intestines and other slimies might edge their way upwards, particularly whilst the body was taking violent exercise. This would certainly make many activities exceedingly uncomfortable and surgery would become an unpredictable matter.

There are various forms of diaphragm in science and engineering, and there seems to be one in my central heating boiler which is far more unreliable than the one that nature provided us with. There is also the kind of diaphragm used in contraception, otherwise called a Dutch cap (why give them the credit?) which is quite easy to use but just as unreliable as the one in the central heating, and I have Sebastian to prove it. When the Pill became available I took to it gladly, willing to endure the occasional headache and assured that as I didn't smoke I ran little risk of thrombosis. The other dire side effects seemed to me to be positively advantageous. I had always been keen to put on a bit of weight (though I didn't) and since I had generally found sex to be an exhausting and repetitive pleasure the reduction of my libido couldn't be a bad thing.

I can't really be sure that my lack of interest in men stemmed from my taking the Pill or from the fact that I find most of them so unattractive. Great fun to talk to but that's the most exciting bit. That's why I got on so well with Bruce. He shared my perspective that sex was interesting but not imperative and we seemed to see the same things as funny. On balance I think we did more talking in bed than anything else. Which is where I made the mistake of expounding to him the details of my idea about writing a personal encyclopaedia.

DIET: the combination of foods we eat, most commonly taken to be the ideal combination necessary to keep a slim body in accordance with one's perception of fashion or health. Julia was very fussy about her diet, for the fashion reason, and would spend much of the time when we sat around the kitchen table scoffing steak and kidney pie and new potatoes or other such luxuries put together by Nancy, sipping unsweetened orange juice or boiling eggs. The minimarket didn't stock the kind of crispbread or pickled fish that her Scandinavianized palate had become used to, so special expeditions had to be made to Bodmin and Truro to seek them out. I realize that it must have been very galling for her to watch me eating pastry and cake and not putting on a pound. She took out her frustations on poor Kate, who was supposed to be building up her strength and therefore conscientiously ate everything that was put before her. As she couldn't take more than the most gentle exercise and as she had recently had her abdominal muscles sliced in two her shape was, to put it kindly, a mess, but none of us had even considered this to be important. When, in the middle of the apple crumble, Julia said directly, 'Kate, when are you going to take yourself in hand?' she hit a very raw nerve. Kate put down her spoon and burst into tears, then pushed back her chair and hobbled out of the room. Joan and Nancy and Jennifer looked embarrassed and Mother said, 'That was rather unnecessary, Julia.'

'All that food is unnecessary,' snorted Julia. 'She's certainly not going to keep Andy in tow with a figure like ... like ...' She glanced around the table at the floppy forms of Nancy and Joan and thought better of what she had been going to say. 'Oh hell, who cares anyway?'

'Kate does,' I suggested. And of course Julia's right. Now that Kate can never be pregnant again, if she loses her looks as well she has nothing to hold Andy. And to her, that's important.

DIRT: matter in the wrong place.

For example, custard in the jug is not dirt; on the carpet it is. There is often a fine perceptual distinction between what is dirt and what is not, which is why so many disputes arise, particularly between children with their infinitely adaptable minds and their elders who tend to be rather set in their thinking on these matters. Mother drew a clear distinction between a child in the outdoors and a child in the house. As soon as it crossed the threshold it was deemed 'dirty' and sent to wash and change its clothes. This really suited everyone quite well for the older children didn't often want to come inside, and when they did it was often water they were seeking anyway.

* * *

DISTANT: a time, place or object that is not near, and thereby often more comfortable and attractive than what you have around you.

DOMINATE: to exert authority or control over others. To be the most important person in a relationship.

It hadn't seemed obvious to me in the early days that Pope had a need to dominate others but either it was always there and drove him to seek the dizzy academic heights of a professor's chair, or the job induced and developed a domineering tendency. At any rate, whenever I wanted to disagree with him I tried to do it in private because in public he would insist on his own way as a matter of course. At first I used to think it was only me who caused these reactions, because of the nature of our past relationship, but gradually I learned that everyone else dealt with him in the same way, particularly after the egg incident.

On the rare occasions when I saw Paula, his poor little wife, mostly at university social functions, it was obvious that the success of their relationship lay in her dominability. I mean, she not so much allowed it as invited it, soaked it up, engorged herself upon it so as to mould herself into a regurgitation of his views and attitudes. If she had ever had a personality of her own it no longer showed.

Did I say 'poor little wife?' That was an error. She was totally and blissfully happy. She was Mrs Professor Pope and could not imagine any greater mission in life.

DOZEN: twelve at a time.

With Julia's arrival it was possible, acknowledging Joan and Nancy as members of the household, to count up to a dozen people in the cottage. This meant the baby as well but this is quite fair since he really did take up a disproportionate amount of attention, what with washing nappies and preparing feeds. The point is that a household of twelve people requires rather more

71

organization in the way of supplies than a household of two, so an arrangement was made with the minimarket that they would deliver most of our goods by the case-load once a week. Everything began to arrive in multiples of a dozen, including the gin.

The baby can't be blamed for the gin consumption but Kate developed quite a taste for it, Mother has always been fond of it, and it was essential in order to offer the Commander a sympathetic berth.

Once I discovered about Gabby's secret activities it didn't surprise me that the Commander often popped round on his own for a quiet couple of drinks but it was some time before I realized that Mother wasn't always entirely pleased to see him. Being the well-mannered person she is she never gave him an inkling of this but one day while I was helping her to lay the supper table she referred to him as 'that soppy old codger' and I asked her what was the matter.

'He's so transparent. Always hinting about how much he likes a lady with old-fashioned virtues and asking me to go out for a sail with him.'

'You, Mother?'

'Whyever not me?' she asked indignantly. 'What makes you think I'm not attractive to . . . well, a certain kind of man?'

'You mean a soppy old codger?'

'Not really, dear. I just got a bit carried away with that figure of speech. The Commander's all right in himself, you know, but he does spend too much time feeling sorry for himself about Gabby.'

'Why should he do that?' I asked cautiously.

'Oh dear, you do miss a lot, closed up in your little study. Surely you can see that Gabby's a young and attractive woman with far too much energy. The Commander's convinced she plays the field a little, and I don't mean cricket.'

'Has he mentioned any names?'

'Names? As though he would be so ungentlemanly!'

*   *   *

DRUG: a substance that affects the central nervous system, either speeding it up or slowing it down, or causing it to malfunction in some way. A lot has been written about the use of drugs in society and the hypocrisy that allows the Commander to drink his gin without censure, and little children to buy and smoke cigarettes, while other innocent pleasures like the smoking of cannabis and the taking of pills have to be outlawed. I just can't follow the moral argument which advocates that because we allow one bad thing we have to allow another. I know all about freedom of choice, too, but the choices are not free for the twelve-year-old who became addicted to nicotine at its mother's knee or behind the bicycle sheds. Neither really are they free for those of us who can't even sit down to write without a strong cup of coffee. So how are they free for a person who can only find pleasure in getting a buzz or taking a trip that may well kill them before too long?

I know it was something stronger than cannabis that left Sebastian shaking and sweating and vomiting, but it was the weed that gave him the taste for alternative sensations. I know that it must have been my fault that he felt so compelled to find some escape route, but why didn't I hear him crying in the night before it was too late to help him? Afterwards my only sensible role was that of jailer; of cleaner of soiled beds and bringer of plastic mugs of water.

7 Eagle—Endive

Progress is being made, but of a slow variety. I've suddenly seen a new angle on some of the data I've got which means that it needs another run through the computer. I made a long phone call to the university computer department, which fortunately never closes down, but the woman who normally deals with my work is on holiday and I had a little difficulty in convincing her substitute that I have the right to use the time. I do have a password but the silly man suggested that I might have stolen it because he's never heard of my name. I could have told him to phone Pope, which would have been unkind because Pope is inclined to be vindictive towards people who disturb him at home unnecessarily, so I sent the man to ask the computer which readily confirmed that it loves and trusts me. But it'll take two days to get time to run the figures and then another day or two for them to reach me by post, so I have to re-jig my work schedule.

EAGLE: a large bird of prey which lives in isolated situations and which flies very high and spots its future meals from a long way off. Hence the phrase 'eagle eye' which means someone who doesn't miss a thing. Like Bassett and the spades.

'Someone's been at me tools,' complained Bassett's face through the kitchen window while we were still breakfasting.

Mother used her favourite defensive ploy. 'Oh dear!

74

Your tools, Mr Bassett? Can you be sure?'

'If I can't, who can?'

'Who indeed. What's happened? Are they missing? Don't you lock them in the shed at night?'

'I do, Ma'am, and they're not. But they been *moved*. They ain't as I left them. They been used and put back again.'

'But is the lock broken?'

'Nope. Been unlocked and locked up again.'

'But who has a key apart from you?'

'You do, Ma'am.'

'You don't really think I indulge in secret overnight gardening, do you?'

Bassett's bright blue eyes wavered. 'No Ma'am, why should you? You pays me. But somebody has, and it's been *heavy* work.'

'Heavy?'

'Spades and forks and the like.'

'And do you see any evidence of heavy digging around the garden anywhere?'

'No, not yet. But I will, you mark my words.' His head disappeared then and we were all left with the feeling that his memory was slipping, that no one could have touched the tools. He'd simply forgotten how he'd put them away. Perhaps he'd had a touch too much cider in the sun. He might be on the warpath but he would find nothing.

EAR: the delicately balanced organ with which we hear.

I make this point about the delicacy of the balance because Pope very nearly destroyed mine when I made the mistake of answering the phone this afternoon. I was nearest at the time and because I had been lulled into a false sense of security I didn't check the reflex of reaching out for the receiver in response to the bell. I'd barely finished giving the number before I was blasted by an angry roar from Pope. 'Sally! What the hell do you think you're doing?'

'Er, trying to enjoy my summer holi . . .'

'I've been trying to trace you all day!'

'How did you manage it?'

'I went round to your flat and found the key you'd so transparently left in the meter cupboard and then this note on the kitchen table with an address and a phone number and something about a dead cat.'

'That was for Sebastian.'

'You really are stupid. Anyone could break in.'

'Did you leave it all the way it was?' If Sebastian wasn't able to trace me if he came home, I'd have to go straight back.

'Leave it? I'm still here.'

'Calling me on *my* phone?'

'Well it's all your fault.'

'What is?'

'Listen Sally, do you or do you not know where Sebastian is?'

My heart gave an extra thump and I was glad Pope couldn't see my face. 'What's that got to do with anything?'

'I want to find him, that's what. I want to put him right about a few things.'

'Nobody can change Sebastian's mind. You know that.'

'It's about time somebody tried. Do you know what he's done?'

Sebastian had done something? Oh wonderful! He could only be alive if he'd done something.

'Well?' barked Pope. 'Do you know?'

'Only if you tell me.'

'He's been writing his own Bruce Wild. He's sent it to me with a covering note saying that as I seem to be the key figure I might as well read it.'

'And did you?'

'Some of it. It's obscene.'

'Really? Can I read it?'

'I can only assume you invented most of it. Someone must have put these ideas into his head.'

'Can't you give him credit for originality?'

'Sally, do you try to infuriate me on purpose?'

Oh no, Pope, it comes quite naturally, I don't have to try at all. 'Pope, will you make sure that you leave my address and phone number exactly where I put them and return my door-key to the meter cupboard? Sebastian hasn't got a key of his own. ' It did seem so important, particularly now that I knew Sebastian was surfacing and returning to sanity.

'Will you tell me where he is?'

'Don't you think you might leave him alone for once? Hasn't he had enough from us? Why don't you send me the Bruce Wild?'

'Certainly not. I'm going to burn it. Paula might see it.'

'Aren't you going to finish reading it first? You never know, the end might be positive.'

'Positive? My God, Sally, I wish you'd had that abortion when I told you.'

He does tend to repeat himself. These days I trust him so little that an hour or two later I rang my neighbour and asked her to check that the key and the note were still where Sebastian could find them.

EARN: to receive something reciprocal in return for work or services, or wrongdoing. You can earn your keep, earn a salary or earn yourself a punishment. It occurs to me that in many of life's situations we manage to do all three by the same set of actions.

EARTH: a name for a planet we live on, or a word to describe the topmost layer of that planet, the one that supports the vegetation. Earth is one substance that is generally regarded as being dirt whether it is in the right place or the wrong place, as evidenced by the use of the word soil as a synonym for earth, because soil also means to make something dirty. Personally I think earth on flower-beds or in fields is quite undirty but on my hands it has a tacky feel and I want to remove it as soon as possible. On children's clothes it is quite noticeably out of place and we really ought to have been warned by the first lot of jeans and shirts that came in for washing that week. I mean, they weren't so much dirty as impossible for the wearers to walk about in any more.

EAT: to take in food through the mouth. Some people see this as a sensual pleasure which takes on a disproportionate significance in their lives, and some people see it as a chore to be executed as quickly and efficiently as possible. Pope and Sebastian are two extremes on this scale. Pope really enjoys good food; when we were students I thought he used to spend far too much money either eating out in restaurants as an occasional treat or buying ingredients for exotic dishes which he would spend hours preparing and hours more eating. I did enjoy the results of his efforts but would never have gone to all that trouble myself. Now that he earns a professor's salary his waistline suggests that the occasional treats in restaurants happen rather more often. I wouldn't be surprised to learn that Paula is an accomplished and careful cook.

On the other hand, Sebastian has never been very interested in food. As a baby he never ate quite as much as the health visitor said he ought to for his weight, he never emptied a cup or a plate or even finished one of those tinned delicacies that promise so much in the way of healthy babies. He never complained about anything he was given and never complained either of being hungry. I think he ate as a matter of social habit because I had trained him to believe it was necessary and he would have been confounded if challenged to give any other reason for ingesting food.

I shouldn't leave this subject without mentioning that Kate now eats very little. After Julia's criticism she didn't have a meal for twenty-four hours, then a bit of shuttle diplomacy from Mother led to her being given a tray on the verandah every mealtime, with enough food to nourish and sustain her but not enough to tempt her to obesity. Julia eats with her, when she's around, though Julia has taken to disappearing for long solitary walks on many days when presumably she eats nothing. She never seems to take any food or money with her. She just strides off towards the cliffs in her smart pants and designer T-shirt with a cashmere cardigan slung across her shoulders.

EBONY: a very hard black wood that comes from tropical forests and has a beautiful surface when polished. I have a little ebony box inlaid with mother-of-pearl in which I keep a curl of Sebastian's baby hair and the first few teeth he exchanged for fivepence pieces (in fact I think I got away with an old sixpence for the first one but they were soon withdrawn and inflation hit that market too). I find it quite a gruesome collection whenever I look at it but I've never had the heart to dispense with it even when I haven't had to wonder whether it might be all I would be left with of Sebastian.

EBULLIENT: a bright, enthusiastic, high-spirited personality. These can be refreshing for a short while but soon become very tiresome, rather like too much ice cream.

ECLIPSE: a covering of one bright planet by the shadow of another. These are astronomical events which occur with predictable regularity and which used to be associated with magical events. I have never seen more than a brief glimpse of an eclipse because every time I have had the opportunity it has been almost totally obscured by cloud. I can't have been more than passingly unfortunate in this respect and yet when you think of the hold that magic has always had on the inhabitants of this murky isle it's hard to understand how eclipses came to be incorporated into supernatural wisdom when they can hardly ever have been noticed.

*   *   *

79

ECONOMIC: the adjective that describes something concerned with finance or wealth, which has usually come to mean either money or other resources used carefully or wisely.

My life with Sebastian was a constant economic struggle for many years because of having to rent a two-person flat in the early stages of my career, and feeling the need to pay for all those little extras, like music lessons and visits and outings, and the canoeing holiday when he nearly drowned himself, and going to the cinema to see films in which I had no interest whatsoever. I knew I could have asked Mother for financial assistance and I suppose I would have done if there'd been some irrevocable disaster, but we always just about managed and it gave me a sense of pride that I'd provided my little son with a warm place to live and a pillow of his own to lay his head on.

However, when Bruce moved in and began to share the household expenses on a 33/66 basis (well, it was my responsibility to provide for Sebastian) things became considerably easier. At about the same time my lecturer's salary edged into a bracket which no longer kept us on the breadline and I bought my first car. It was a ropey little old thing, but despite all the odd bits that fell off from time to time it somehow kept on the road and I shall never forget the sense of freedom and relief at not having to wait for buses or rush to catch trains, and at being able to take Sebastian and Bruce out into the country.

It was pretty good having Bruce around in those days because he was funny and undemanding and didn't expect to make all my decisions for me, and he and Sebastian were so happy in each other's company. They even went off on a holiday together when Sebastian was fifteen, one summer when I had a couple of weeks' summer school tutoring to do for the Open University. Bruce took Sebastian to stay with some friends of his who lived on a croft in Scotland. The train fares were rather

80

expensive but I was earning good money at the summer
school so I didn't mind.

EEL: a long, snakelike fish; well, not always very long.
Some of them can be quite large but the ones the children brought to show us swimming around in the bucket
were only a few inches long. They had come upon a
fisherman using them for bait and had managed to rescue these few while he was busy landing his catch.
Mother suggested that this was stealing but Miranda
pointed out that he had stolen them from their homes
and families in the first place, so it couldn't really count.
Kate took one look and retreated to the verandah,
clutching the baby.

'But what are you going to do with them?' Mother
wanted to know.

'Throw them away this instant,' called Kate.

'Oh no, please.' Melly's eyes filled with tears.

'They really should go back into the sea,' said
Miranda.

'Do they come from the sea?'

'Oh yes,' Roger said. 'They're in salt water. I tasted it.'
Kate shuddered.

'I want to keep them as pets,' insisted Melly.

'But we don't know what to feed them on.'

'We could go and ask . . . you know . . . Aunt Julia's
friend.' They exchanged knowing looks.

'Aunt Julia's friend?' Mother asked, retreating to her
embroidery.

'A person in the village Aunt Julia talks to sometimes.'

'He knows all about fishing.'

'Trouble is, he may want them for bait as well.'

'We don't have any choice,' said Miranda. 'They'll die
anyway if we keep them in this bucket without food.'

'I won't *let* anyone stick hooks into them,' Melly
insisted as they set off. The last phrase we heard as they
drifted across the lawn was from Roger. 'Hey, maybe we
could put them in the . . .' He was hastily nudged by the

two girls who glanced anxiously over their shoulders at us.

'In the bath?' Kate wondered, arranging the baby on her knee. 'No, they wouldn't dare!'

I was more intrigued with the question of whether the fastidious Julia could really be interested in a smelly rogue like Potter, and what Gabby was doing about it.

EFFICIENT: the organization of time or resources so as to achieve the greatest possible effect for the least possible input. It is not easy to be efficient, or to know if one is being inefficient, unless someone points it out to you. I think that on the whole I organize my time fairly productively these days but Julia has been concerned enough to point out that if I spent less time hunched over a typewriter and more time and money on my appearance I could quite easily find myself a supportive male and then I wouldn't need to work so hard. Either she is being deliberately offensive or she just doesn't understand that we are running in different races.

ELECTRICITY: a form of power generated by friction, magnetism or heat, which disturbs the molecular structure of bodies. This power can then be sent charging along cables or through the atmosphere, causing sparks to fly and civilization to develop. I know a bit about this through helping Sebastian with his homework. He was quite good at physics before his mind slipped out of gear altogether.

EMANCIPATE: to free from restrictions, either of a physical or conceptual nature.

The Commander was very fond of talking about Gabby's 'emancipation' which he said had first attracted him to her, but which made her very difficult to live with.

'Of course I know you're an emancipated woman too, but not in the same way as Gabby is.' It was me he had caught up with this time, not Mother. I was glad he could see a difference between Gabby's sort of freedom and mine. 'I so admired the way she did exactly as she pleased, never mind what anyone thought. I was so proud of her spirit.' He sounded as though he was talking about some kind of pet animal.

'Is that why you asked her to marry you?'

'I didn't, oh no, I didn't. I would never have presumed. After all, how could I expect that she would be interested in anything so conventional as marriage?'

'A lot of people are.'

'But I mean, she could have had *anybody*. No, she asked me to marry her. I must admit I was shattered by the idea.'

'You didn't have to agree to it.'

'I couldn't have refused. You are so practical, Sally, don't you understand what it's like to fall in love? To be unable to resist any whim, however far-fetched it may seem?'

'I've heard that it does happen to people.' Had I been in love with Bruce? I'd certainly been unable to tell him to go when I should have done but I'd convinced myself that it was because his companionship meant so much to Sebastian. 'Why did Gabby decide she wanted to get married?'

'I have wondered about it. I think she was bored and hard up, and she'd just been dropped from the cricket team for not turning up at the nets once too often. It was right in the middle of their Far Eastern tour and they were going to send her home to England. That didn't agree with her at all. May I help myself to another drink?' He did so without waiting for my assent.

'If you don't like her . . . emancipation, why don't you do something about it?'

'Did I say I didn't like it? No no, that's not the point. She goes off and has her little flings and she's as happy as can be. All charm and sunshine in the home. I know people talk a bit but if it wasn't that they'd find something else. You get very accustomed to gossip after a life in the Services. No, what makes it difficult is when she gets put out. You know, thrown over, usurped. Then she's impossible to live with. I can't bear to be in the house with her right now. It's sulks and snaps and constantly changing her mind about what she's going to do next and what she wants me to do. Impossible!'

'She's been usurped, has she?'

'Oh definitely. I know the signs immediately. If I knew who the fellow was I'd go and punch his nose for him. It's no way to treat a lady!'

EMPTY: not full up, totally without contents. Like my glass, which the Commander promptly replenished before going on to tell me about a time he had stitched up a gash in the hand of a rating who had been careless with a kitchen knife. He had put in twelve stitches and been so proud of the job, only to be told by the doctor who checked the wound later that two would have been sufficient.

ENDIVE: a form of curly-leaved vegetable grown in warmer climes, often used in salad. This sticks clearly in my mind because I was washing endive for yesterday's supper, doing it very carefully because Nancy had told me that a friend of hers had found a Colorado beatle in one a few days before. If I found one I was to put it in a screw-topped jar and phone the police, who presumably were more interested in stray beetles than stray dogs. Nancy was so well organized that she'd even left an appropriate jar on the draining board, just in case. While I was attending to the endive I saw out of the corner of my eye, through the window, a very odd couple turning in through the gate from the lane. I'm ashamed that recognition wasn't instant but both the timing and nature of the apparition were so unexpected. What I saw first was a wheelchair in which sat a plump, dark girl with a small suitcase across her knees. Pushing the wheelchair, and hunched beneath the burden of a large rucksack, was Sebastian.

8 Fable—Funny

I didn't know how to react once I had mopped my first instinctive onrush of tears. I stayed where I was and let Jennifer open the door. Sebastian's first words were, 'Have you got room for us?' and she was about to send them away saying that we didn't do bed and breakfast when Mother came down the stairs and exclaimed, 'There you are! We've been wondering when you were going to arrive.'

'Hello Gran, this is Selena. She's my Control,' Sebastian said as he bumped the wheelchair into the hall.

'Hello Selena. Why didn't you let us know you were coming? I'd have met you in the car.'

The girl in the wheelchair said something and Sebastian asked, 'Where's Mum?'

Mother must have pointed because he appeared in the kitchen doorway and I was glad I'd waited. I was choked as though I was greeting a long-lost lover. He hesitated a moment, perhaps expecting anger, then he stepped forward and we hugged in a way that we hadn't since he was tiny. There was a difference about him: the unfamiliar beginnings of a beard; a rosy tinge to his cheeks. 'I'm back, Mum.'

'Where from?'

'I will tell you later, but not now.'

It was the nearest thing to a conversation we'd had for a long time and I had to make do with it. I imagined that 'later' would come quite soon, but later it really was.

*   *   *

FABLE: a narrative fiction, generally allegorical or moralistic in nature. If this was a fable I think the moral might be 'You can't win many of them,' but of course this narrative is true.

FACE: the front part of the head, which contains most of the organs of communication and by which we are most generally recognized. For a few days I found it quite difficult to get used to Sebastian's face again. The chin stubble was shaved off once he was organzied to buy a razor. He smiled quite a lot and his once dulled eyes had a lively twinkle.

I was very anxious not to make things difficult for him, or for Selena either if he wanted her with him. It was Mother who made the enquiry as to whether they wanted a room together, which surprised me considering that at one time she found it difficult to reconcile herself to putting Bruce and me in the same room when we visited her. Perhaps that was because she hadn't liked Bruce, whereas she seemed to have an instant affection for Selena. It was just as well that Selena said, 'Yes, we must stay together. Sebastian's my Control,' because there was only one free room anyway. To have put them separately would have meant reorganizing the children's sleeping arrangements and although they hadn't slept indoors for weeks Kate kept hoping that one morning she would find them tucked up in their little beds once again.

FACTORY: a place where goods are mass-produced, thereby keeping our consumer society supplied with consumables and the workers supplied with money to buy the consumables they are producing. Sebastian had worked in a factory, the only job he ever did, while he was supposed to be in college studying to retake his 'O' levels. I didn't know he wasn't going to the college until the end of term when I received a rather shirty letter from them pointing out that he had only made a total of fifteen half-day attendances out of a possible eighty-two. That was less than one whole day a week and I thought it must have taken some effort to keep himself away so often. I only found out about the factory when they phoned up to give him the sack because of all the days he took off, presumably to smoke away the money he had earned on his days on. By that time there was no communication between us at all but I still thought he was into nothing more dangerous than hash.

FAIR: light-coloured hair or complexion; something not as good as it could be but not bad either; an even-handed situation, favouring all parties equally. You have to be an optimist to expect life to be fair.

I complained of unfairness to Bruce when I realized he was using my idea to develop a counselling therapy and write his PhD thesis.

'It might be your idea,' he retorted, 'but who's doing it? Who's worked out how to analyse the therapeutic value? Who's applied for the grant to get the research assistants?'

'That's all very well, but I could have done that if you'd suggested to me that it might be useful.'

'The world is full of people who have good ideas but can't see how to use them. You've only got yourself to blame.'

FALLACY: something that is believed to be true but is based on false reasoning. For instance, that friends and lovers help each other.

FAMILY: a group of people closely genetically related to each other. Animals too, I suppose. But not to be confused, as Joey does, happily supposing that he is a full and equal member of our family.

Mother made tactful enquiries about Selena's family, wondering how long she was going to be with us. It turns out she hasn't got one any more. Her mother died of cancer when she was a young child and her father and aunt were killed in the car accident that left her with a severed spinal cord. 'I'm her family now,' Sebastian told us.

FAST: three meanings, I think. To go without eating; to tie something up so that it won't come undone; to move or accomplish something quickly.

I could talk about Kate's dietary regime, which is having good visual effect and is actually making her more lively. I could talk about the fact that Julia has taken to practising nautical knots. But uppermost in everyone's mind today is the speed with which the children accomplished their latest project.

It took us all by surprise except, in a way, Bassett, who had been convinced that something was afoot. The surreptitious night-time use of the tools must have been some preparatory work, carefully concealed, though how they had stolen Mother's key and undone and re-locked the door was a mystery that no one had time to go into with the other recriminations that were being bandied about. What greeted us all in the morning, and we were alerted to by a roar from Bassett, was a stream, or ditch, cut neatly across the lawn and through the vegetable garden, carrying water from the village stream past the children's camp in the orchard and out into a ditch that was part of the neighbouring farmer's land drain system. There was nobody in the household who wasn't totally amazed as we all slowly crossed the lawn and surveyed this marvel of engineering. Without disturbing anyone the three elder children had dug it and got the water flowing during the course of the night, unaided by adult hand as far as we could tell, although some of us did have our suspicions.

'That's it!' cried Bassett as he picked up his lunch bag. 'That's sabotage, mean and deliberate. I'm not coming back no more!'

We were all too stunned to try to persuade him otherwise. Kate was already storming off towards the orchard when three dirty, sleepy faces appeared above the hedge. They had the grace to look very anxious.

'What did you do it for?' shouted Kate. 'I ask you, what for?'

They all emerged slowly. 'We needed water in our camp.'

'You're always complaining that we're dirty. We wanted to be able to wash.'

'What was wrong with the bathroom?'

'We wanted to wash out of doors.'

'Didn't you know it was a naughty thing to do?'

'We thought you might stop us, that's why we did it in secret . . .'

'But we thought it might look so nice that you'd like it afterwards.'

'Well we don't like it! Get inside the house, all of you, this minute!'

Kate pointed to the house, then swung round to face us, looking for support. I heard a strange sound at my elbow and found that Mother was struggling to control laughter. Kate's jaw dropped. The children looked even more anxious: dissension amongst the adults was more than they'd bargained for.

'Why is it funny?' Julia asked. 'These children have been deliberately headlong and destructive.'

'No, they haven't,' Mother said. 'They've been determined and enterprising. Isn't that right, Sally?'

That's the way I would have seen it if it had been Sebastian. 'Just think of the effort they've put in.'

'And it really will look quite pretty when Sebastian's landscaped it,' suggested Selena in her husky voice.

Kate sulked and retreated to the safety of caring for the baby. The children came into the kitchen and had an enormous breakfast, then retired to their tent and slept all day. They celebrated that evening by having a bath in their stream.

*   *   *

FILIAL: feelings or attitudes appropriate from a child to its parent.

'I'm not surprised you didn't tell me about that weirdo being my father,' Sebastian wrote from Scotland. 'I'd have been ashamed too if I couldn't have provided a child of mine with anything better. You creep around the whole time trying to please him, and I can tell he wants me to do the same, but I won't. He's always trying to put me right about things. If I had to have a father like that why couldn't you have lost him long ago instead of letting him lurk about on the sidelines trying to interfere?'

There was a lot more in that vein and what troubled me most at the time was how Sebastian had found out. I could only suppose that Bruce had told him, but how did Bruce know? And how could he think of telling Sebastian without talking to me about it first?

When I cooled down I telephoned Pope to find out if he'd broken his promise. He hadn't said anything to Sebastian, but he had told Bruce.

'When? Why?'

'Oh, when I knew you were living together. It only seemed fair to warn him.'

And all Bruce would say was, 'I thought he ought to know. You shouldn't keep information like that from kids.' When I tried to express my anger I was told, 'You fuss too much, Sally dear. It'll be all right, you'll see.'

FILM: a thin layer of transparent material. Celluloid film is the substance used to record photographic images and so the word has come to be synonymous with the strip of images which become a moving film.

Sven makes films, which is why he has a lot of money to spend on Julia. When I say he makes them, I mean he organizes and directs them. The kind he is most successful with are the classy travelogues which sell to television companies. Sven films beautiful places and then writes a script which is translated into several languages and voiced over the film, thereby providing him with an international market. That's how Julia came upon him, by auditioning to dub the English script. She had set out in life as a reporter for a regional TV company. She got the job and got the glamorous film director as well.

I mention all this because Sven arrived yesterday evening, when Kate and Mother were playing bridge at the Forresters' and Julia was elsewhere. Sebastian and Selena were sitting near the open verandah doors, playing chess. I had checked that the children were in camp and sat down to read a book. Jennifer had gone out to spend the evening at her own home. Life was pretty peaceful. Something was bound to happen.

The high-powered engine, the car door slamming, the quick ring on the bell put me in mind of Andy first and I thought how like him to take us by surprise when he'd put off coming at the planned times. I opened the door and found a tight-lipped and sunken-eyed Sven. I took him straight into the kitchen because I thought he needed sustenance. He was quite keen on the idea of whisky and he sat and sighed into his glass while I made him some sandwiches and wondered again how such an utterly beautiful man could exist. His skin was golden, his hair blond, his eyes bright blue, his features like those of a Michelangelo statue. I think his body probably matched but I had never seen much of it. As I watched him tears rolled down his cheeks.

'Well, you seem not to be surprised to see me, but Julia is not here then?' More whisky into the glass.

'She is, but she's not just now. How long have you been looking for her?'

'Since I found her gone. Yesterday, day before? I get home from working in Germany and find this letter.' More whisky. 'She has gone away for ever. She finds me too much! How am I too much? I am hardly there!'

That, I think, might have been Julia's complaint, in more ways than one. I pushed across a box of tissues for Sven to wipe his eyes and blow his nose. 'Never mind, Sven.' More whisky.

'She has her house, her clothes, her car, her time to herself and that is not enough! I ask her, what else is it you want my darling and she says children, Sven, but how can we make children when she is so cold that I cannot respond to her?'

Julia said he was cold, he said she was. I knew she was warm enough right at that moment. But I didn't know about Sven.

I sat down opposite him while he soaked up some of the whisky with my sandwiches. 'Sven, do you have a girlfriend or anything?'

'Me? A girl? You think maybe that's why Julia has gone? No one, Sally, I swear. She has no cause to complain.'

I sat and listened to him crying and talking for an hour or so and wondered what Julia was up to. She must have left this address behind her because otherwise he would never have found her so quickly, which meant she must have wanted him to follow her. But now she was having if off with Potter: it was impossible to ignore the faint smell of fish that clung to her from time to time. Was she merely amusing herself or trying to make a point for Sven who she knew would turn up sooner or later to take her home?

When she did come in, around midnight, she took one furious look at her husband and shouted at me, 'He can't stay here!'

'He can't go anywhere else tonight.' It would have been criminal to let him drive the car.

'It's okay,' Sven burbled. 'I go to a hotel. I come back tomorrow.'

'No hotels here, and you don't come back at all!' Julia was screaming, rather unnecessarily, I thought. 'I'm fed up with your inhibited northern manners and all that snow! I'm not going to be taken home like a naughty schoolgirl!'

There was a problem because Selena and Sebastian had taken the last room and if Julia wouldn't have Sven with her—oh yes, one of the children's beds. It was Sebastian who guided the poor weeping fellow upstairs with much cooing and clucking and settled him down. He had gone before breakfast the next morning.

FINAL: the last part of anything, the ending. It could be said that nothing is ever final because one thing always leads to another.

FINANCE: to do with money. I've already dealt with this under 'economic'.

FIRE: combustion caused by heat or friction. There was a fire on the downland above the cliff, only half a mile from the village. They said it was caused by a cigarette end dropped by a walker and if there'd been much of a wind blowing it would have threatened the cottages before the nearest fire engine arrived. The children were with Potter on the beach at the time, luring tourists into his boat and selling souvenirs. As soon as the fire was spotted he sent them home and immediately gathered up a group of helpers and went up the path to beat out the flames. He was slightly burned going into a copse to save a snared badger that was hanging half dead from a tree. Afterwards Julia drove him to the nearest hospital to have his burns dressed and she didn't come home at all that night. Sebastian told us that some very angry words passed between the locals in the pub that evening and for several days afterwards the village simmered with bad feeling.

FISH: aquatic creatures, varying in size from the very small to the very large, and mostly good to eat. They have a very distinctive smell, but I've already mentioned that too.

FLOWER: the blossom of a plant containing all the reproductive seed-producing parts. Flowers are usually, though not always, very brightly coloured and beautiful

93

so that they can attract the insects that carry out the pollination. We humans, in our wisdom, cultivate them for their beauty to delight our eyes. This has nothing to do with Nature's Plan because flowers appear in profusion in places where people never go, whether we do anything about it or not.

The garden of the cottage is one of those in which attention has been paid to encouraging a succession of flowers of one sort or another at every season. Sebastian pointed this out to me. I had always thought the garden looked nice but Sebastian showed me the chrysanthemums and the winter jasmine, and pointed out the way the different seasons' flowers were arranged in a kind of rotation around the garden, early and late ones being placed in positions where they would get the maximum amount of sun.

I was surprised that he knew so much about it. He'd had his early interest in growing things, of course, until I destroyed his cannabis experiment, and after Bassett left us he really took over. Baskets of fat fresh vegetables appeared without anyone having to ask for them, the lawn was mown before anyone noticed it was needed, and within a few days of the stream appearing its banks were sprouting water plants and were flanked here and there by rockeries that changed the level and interspersed the flow with little waterfalls. He said the water was a positive benefit to the vegetable garden.

Selena worked in the garden too. She would be lifted out of her wheelchair to sit on the edge of the lawn so that she could weed and fuss over the plants. She had thick, powerful shoulders that enabled her to drag her useless legs behind her and, although she couldn't go very fast, she was quite mobile. Mother took to bringing out a little mat and working beside her, talking to her. Kate was a bit put out by this because she had had the advantage of most of Mother's conversation up to now, sitting on the verandah. But Kate hated gardening and I think Mother was beginning to find babies a limited subject for discourse. It was noticeable that Kate began to find other things to do and even took the baby out for short walks along the lane in a hired pram.

FOLIAGE: the leafy part of a plant, not always as attractive as the flower, but more enduring, and doing a basic job in the survival process by providing nourishment.

FOX: a dog-like wild animal with a beautiful reddish brown coat and a face that is either appealing or sly, depending on whether you are a naturalist or a farmer who has just had his chickens raided. Despite being hunted and shot at for centuries foxes have survived and even moved into urban environments, thus showing very human characteristics.

FOOD: the substances we eat to fuel our bodies. Some of us over-stoke ourselves, as Julia pointed out to Kate, others of us seem to need more fuel per hour. Selena has to be very careful not to over-eat because she is unable to take much exercise, whereas Sebastian now consumes an incredible amount which I find quite interesting in view of his past lack of interest. They sit side by side at mealtimes, she encouraging him to eat more, he reminding her when she has had enough. I begin to get an insight into the meaning of their cryptic comments that each is the other's 'control'.

FUNNY: 'Haha or peculiar?' we used to say when we were children. It can mean something that makes us laugh, and I think it's true that no one has yet come up with a satisfactory explanation of why some things make some people laugh while others stare coldly; nor yet of the physiological purpose of laughter.

Funny peculiar is really using the word as a synonym for 'strange', as when the Commander said, 'Funny thing, Gabby found a Scandinavian wandering round

95

the village yesterday, looking for somewhere to stay. Of course there's nothing vacant at the moment so she brought him home to us. Rather good-looking fellow. Says he's looking for his wife.'

9   Gag—Gullible

GAG: something placed over the mouth to prevent speech, or a joke. I really can't see the connection between the two as in order to make a gag you certainly cannot be gagged.

GALANTINE: a dish of cold meat in a savoury jelly. I had always considered this a rather fancy form of food but Nancy makes particularly good galantine with no apparent effort. She was in the process of doing one of these when we had the first hint of trouble in the kitchen. Selena, it seems, is very fond of cooking as well as of gardening, but Nancy didn't appreciate her presence 'cluttering up the space' and told her so. Joan was rather shocked at the idea of rejecting a handicapped person like this. I think we were all a little uneasy about it at first, not knowing whether to refer to it directly, or whether to make allowances or not. It soon became obvious that we were more sensitive than Selena was and after a while nobody gave it a second thought, specially as Sebastian deals with all the real difficulties, such as bathing and toilets and getting up and down stairs. The only times he is further than a room away from her needs is when he goes on his early morning jogs. Yes, Sebastian, the lethargic, the undisciplined, waking up early and jogging for miles! He returns flushed and lively, makes cups of tea, then helps Selena through her ablutions, into her clothes and down for breakfast. Why does he do so much for her? I suppose he loves her.

There's a sort of peacefulness about him I've never seen before. And she makes him laugh.

GALAXY: a grouping of stars or planets which form part of the universe. Our galaxy is called, by us, the Milky Way and consists of numbers of stars, and distances, that stretch the imagination beyond endurance. I mean, once you begin thinking seriously in those realms, mere earthbound problems seem superfluous. It would be quite easy after a while to lose touch with reality. Yes, I know our galaxy is reality as much as my next cup of coffee, but somehow I can get along without knowing about it.

GALLEON: a sixteenth century sailing ship, equipped for fighting as well as for commerce. Commander Forrester is very knowledgeable about sailing ships, past and present, and will talk about them for hours if you make the mistake of allowing him to begin. He must have been rather frustrated, having to confine his naval career to engine-driven ships, because it's obvious that he's at his happiest when he's bobbing around on the estuary in his little sailing boat. He goes out nearly every day. It's easy to see him because he has bright red sails.

Gabby never goes with him. She says, 'It's boring just bobbing around out there. I wish he'd get a boat that would really go somewhere.'

GALLOP: the fast running pace of a horse, but also refers to a lop-sided leaping/running movement in humans. Sebastian has to gallop when he wants to run because the accident with the swimming pool roof left him with one leg very slightly shorter than the other. When he sets off with Selena at speed along the flat sand by the water's edge, the galloping sets up a rocking motion in the wheelchair and Selena clings to the armrests and shrieks with laughter. Sebastian gets caught in the fine spray thrown up by the wheels of the chair and ends up drenched as well as breathless. Thankfully most of their progress is safer than that and the village has become used to the sight of the buxom Selena hunched in the chair with the long, dour Sebastian bent over her as they limp their way to the pub for a drink or to the post office to cash their social security checks.

GAMBLE: to lay out a stake in the hope of getting a multiplied return as the result of chance. It's usually money, but people sometimes gamble with their property or their lives or other people's feelings.

GARRET: a room at the top of a house, often where work proceeds, such as mine. The computer printouts came back a week after I'd sent the stuff in and I was right about the possible new connection I'd spotted. You see, I'm trying to isolate and analyse all the different background factors that may contribute to success and failure of counselling in the self-help family therapy unit. The problem with calling a study like this 'finished' is that new ideas crop up every time I look at the data and reports. Having so many distractions recently must have jolted my thoughts out of a particular rut and onto a fresh, less cluttered pathway. The problem is, what further new insights are possible? I don't suppose I'll ever get it right, just come to the most reasonable conclusion at the time of writing. There's sure to be someone else who'll come along afterwards and correct my results.

GARDEN: a plot of land that is cultivated. I've already said quite a lot about the cottage garden but this seems an appropriate point to mention that Mother told me that Selena has told her that Sebastian learned a lot about gardening at the Centre.

'Centre of what?'

'This place where he's been working. Didn't he tell you? Selena says that's where they met. They were assigned to one another, she says.'

*   *   *

99

GENIAL: a cheerful, pleasant personality.

The Commander is a genial person, and so is Peter Potter, and the Rector as well. Joan and Nancy are genial, though I notice that Joan is a little tight-lipped these days. The children are genial and so is Selena. Now the interesting thing about this list is the people I know who are not on it, and the only reason I can think of for their being on the other side of the line is that they let their complications hang out, or perhaps it's just that I know them better so they can't hide from me. Perhaps that's what geniality is: a veil that hides people from each other.

GESTURE: a motion of the body or arms with which people address each other. I am very interested in this particular form of body language, which I reckon is more significant in interpersonal interactions than speech or eye contact. I've devoted a lot of time to reading about the use of gesture between people, and I've dreamed up a scheme for a study based on initiating casual conversations and then finding out from the participants what they thought they were doing with their hands while they were talking. Pope doesn't think it's very important. He says that the subject's already been well covered by the anthropologists and he doesn't see that a sociologist can add anything worthwhile. I watched the way he pressed his fingers together while he was talking and decided to continue with my study next year.

GHASTLY: a thing or event that is horrifying, or extremely unpleasant.

I can't think of anything I personally found ghastly until I knew that Sebastian was taking heroin. Then I had to try to face up to it. I needed someone to turn to and nobody was there. Pope was all anger by that time and Bruce had gone. Mother was away cruising in the Caribbean with Julia and pretending not to notice Julia's escapades with sultry stewards. I crept around our home, keeping the curtains closed to contain my empty misery within the walls of the flat. I tried to look after Sebastian. I fed him and held him and finally fought with him, but I couldn't prevent him from going out again and he didn't come back until he'd run out of money. Was that only last summer? Was it only a year that I'd been hawking him around hospitals and clinics like a once saleable item that I could no longer give away?

GOOSEBERRY: a sharp-tasting fruit that grows on prickly bushes and makes into very fine pie. There is a rumour that babies used to be left under gooseberry bushes to be found by their parents, rather than being born in the conventional manner. This was invented by prudish Victorians who preferred not to talk about sex or to connect anything so monstrous with something as innocent as a baby. Fortunately this myth (about the gooseberry bush, not about sex being connected with babies) is dying out because modern children learn about sex and babies very early in their lives, though often the next thing they learn is not to talk to their parents about it. I don't remember ever mentioning it to Mother. Part of the truth came from other girls at school, part from books, and the rest through inspired guesswork. I remember trying to make things easier for Julia, who was a few years younger than me, when she started at senior school. I explained to her what it was all about and she flatly refused to believe me. She insisted, 'I can remember Kate being born and Mother wasn't at all fat and we went to the hospital to get her.'

'She was enormous.' My memory was clearer. 'And she went to the hospital to *have* Kate.'

'No, it can't be true, it's too horrible,' Julia exclaimed tearfully so I left her to her innocence. I don't know who told Kate, but she was young enough to be a member of that generation who knew all about it from a very early age. I resolved that there would be no such inhibitions between Sebastian and myself. When I received a letter from his primary school to say that they were being shown a series of sex education films I went along to the parents' evening beforehand and made every effort to discuss it with him afterwards, but he seemed to find the whole subject rather boring. As far as I was aware he never showed any interest in girls. I did try to be discreet about sexual activity with Bruce, in case it disturbed him, but I later realized that nothing could have shaken Sebastian's belief that Bruce only lived with us in order to provide companionship for him.

GRAVITY: the centrifugal force that keeps us all pinned to the surface of the planet and which, as the children well know, makes cricket balls come back to earth and water run down the slightest of gradients, and people sometimes fall down cliffs.

Julia said she had slipped whilst walking along the cliff path, watching the Commander's little red sails bobbing about in the distance. Roger told me she slipped on her way down from the caves and serve her right too because they'd told her that I'd told them it was dangerous to go up there. Her physical injuries at first seemed slight—a twisted ankle and a very nasty graze along the entire length of one beautiful leg—but I think she felt very undignified coming a cropper in front of the children. It seems that they were scolding her and trying to help her to her feet when Potter appeared and she had no choice but to allow him to carry her home. Potter must have been dismayed to watch her fall and to have to choose between leaving her unaided and allowing the children to see him following her down from the cave. I think he managed that bit quite well, while the children were distracted, and he seemed to be rather enjoying the situation by the time they arrived at the cottage, followed by the entourage of Miranda, Roger, Melly and Joey, who all mysteriously disappeared as soon as Mother and Kate took over and began bathing and bandaging. Mother offered Potter a cup of tea but he said he had to get back to his boat to prepare for the evening's trip.

'Lobster pots,' he explained. 'Any of you ladies care to come along?'

Julia shot him a filthy look as he winked at Mother and said, 'What about you, Mrs Fry? How'd you fancy a sunset outing?'

Mother laughed, I'm sure because the idea at that moment seemed too preposterous. I shuddered because being afloat at all just doesn't appeal to me. Kate stuck her nose in the air but had the grace to mutter something about not being well enough at present for those kind of jaunts. Potter shrugged and went on his way and Julia hobbled to the couch, weeping with rage and frustration at the thought of what a few days' being laid up might do to her personal life. In fact it turned out to be worse than a few days. By the following morning the twisted ankle was swollen to twice its size so I drove her to the hospital in Truro where they took X-rays and then put the whole foot in plaster.

GRUDGE: having a feeling that someone has done you some harm or injury, and you feeling resentful about it and meaning to get your own back sometime.

I think I felt like this towards Bruce's thesis when I found out what it was about and I suppose from that point the specific grudge began to generalize to the rest of our relationship. At any rate, somehow his bright flowered shirts began to seem affected and his humour a trifle condescending. I became aware of something a little false about his whole style.

GRAVY: a brown sauce made from the juices of meats. I'm quite a passable cook, of necessity, but I've never been very good with gravy. It tends to go into lumps or if it's smooth it's too thin and watery. Selena showed me how to make it by browning the flour in a pan and then slowly adding dripping and liquid to it, which was completely the opposite way to how I'd been taught, and which certainly solved the problem and makes the best gravy I've ever tasted. That was later, though, after she'd taken complete charge of the kitchen.

GRUMPY: a sour and dissatisfied frame of mind which results in being mildly bad tempered with other people. Bassett had been grumpy, but he was no longer with us, except that he sometimes strolled down the lane and leaned on the gate, passing the time of day and prognosticating fearfully about what the owners of the cottage would say when they saw what had been done to their property. Nancy was definitely becoming more grumpy than she had been and I could see that the increasing numbers in the household and their disorganized way of life must be putting a strain on her that she wasn't prepared for. Gabby was grumpy for a while after Julia's arrival but she seems quite happy again now.

The Commander was very grumpy with Mother for having her hair cut. It came about one day when Mother offered to take Selena to Plymouth to buy some clothes. Selena was greatly excited by the idea and even communicated some enthusiasm to Sebastian, who had to go too even though Mother was sure she could manage Selena's chair by herself.

The shopping trip was certainly a success from the point of view that both Selena and Sebastian came back with some badly needed new clothes. But none of us was too sure about what had happened to Mother. I mean, we could all see what had happened but it was difficult to decide whether it was a success. The effect was so total. Mother's long silver hair had been cut short and curled gently around her face. And instead of her neat linen suit and court shoes she was wearing a pair of pale green dungarees which looked rather striking with a new cream silk blouse, her pearls, and canvas shoes. I'm afraid she was greeted by a stunned silence every time she encountered a member of the household but she was too pleased with herself to be put out.

'You really are a lot of fuddy-duddies,' she scolded. 'Just wait till you see me in my red boiler suit.'

At first we all thought it had been an underhand plot but it transpired that soon after their arrival in Plymouth Sebastian, true to form, had upset a cup of coffee over Mother. Not just a slight upset, but a whole cup, from head to toe. Something had to be done about it and it had not taken much encouragement from Selena to bring out the new image. I suppose that if one of us had been with her we would have gently disparaged her glances towards these uncharateristics clothes, and we would never have discovered that all the time a very raffish person has been lurking near to the surface of our serene and dignified mother.

The Commander was very disapproving when he popped round for his drink that evening. 'Is nothing sacred?' he asked me. 'Ruining a beautiful image like that! Does everything have to be brash and modern?'

'I didn't do it,' I pointed out.

'No, I've heard. It was your irresponsible son and that strange girl of his. You really shouldn't have let them take your mother off like that.'

GUERILLA: a secret fighter who infiltrates and attacks in a stealthy way rather than going for an open battle. There are jungle guerillas, rural guerillas and urban guerillas these days in our vocabulary of warfare, and now it seems that Sven has become a village guerilla.

It was Sebastian who used the phrase, pointing out that he was often lurking around corners or disappearing into the distance, but that he never spoke to any of us. I must say I had thought it odd that he hadn't been seen, even though a full two weeks had elapsed since he'd moved in with the Forresters. I could understand why he didn't want to come round to the cottage but I would have expected to catch sight of him from time to time if he was in the village. Alerted by Sebastian's comment I kept a better lookout as I went about and I, too, began to catch fleeting glimpses of a lone figure clad in flappy shorts and shirt and gym shoes, and carrying a pair of binoculars. He would be moving away along the road, or just going into a shop, or climbing a hill in the middle distance. Once I was certain I saw him ducking behind a hedge. The dark glasses and straw hat he wore made him look even more furtive, but convinced me that this really was Sven and I could only conclude that he was spying on us, or more particularly Julia.

GULLIBLE: easily convinced of what other people want you to believe. I've already told how gullible I was about Sebastian's cannabis plant and my gullibility extended to having faith that Bruce's presence was good for Sebastian. I've often asked myself what else I could have believed, what signs I might have missed in my efforts to convince myself that what I liked was best for us both. What I didn't begin to see until too late were the causes rather than the results of the relationship.

My first enlightenment came one afternoon when I'd come home unexpectedly after a lecture had been cancelled. In my years as a social worker I'd become fairly familiar with the sickly sweetish smell that pervaded the flat and it took only a moment to track it down to Sebastian's room.

Sebastian smiled at me through the haze while I opened the window, then he offered me his joint. I snatched it and ground it out in the wet wash basin. 'Aw Mum, why did you do that?' he wailed, and burst into tears.

'You should be in school,' I pointed out rather foolishly.

'Yes, sure. I'll go now.' He scrambled to his feet and reached for his jacket but I pushed him back.

'Don't be stupid.'

'But I thought you wanted me to go?'

'Sebastian, we've got to talk about this!'

'Yes?' He sat looking up at me, smiling again, mild and

106

complaisant, so unlike the Sebastian I was used to dealing with.

'This sort of thing has got to stop.'

'Oh yes, it will Mum, don't worry. It will.'

'You've got to do something positive to help yourself. I can't keep a watch on you all the time.'

'No, I know you can't.'

'I'll tell you what, though. Suppose we go away for a holiday together when term ends? It's only another couple of weeks. We could take a long break right away from here and get you out of this stupid habit.'

'That sounds like a great idea. Can Bruce come along too?'

'If he wants to. It'll be fun with the new car.'

'Okay Mum, good thinking.'

'Now let me get you something to eat.'

'Good old Mum. Always getting me things to eat.'

'I'm not old yet. But I feel it when you do things like this. You know you'll get picked up by the police again and they won't let you off lightly this time.'

'Don't worry Mum. I'm much more careful now.'

'Oh God, how often does this go on? Have you got any more of that stuff here?'

'No, I'm cleaned out. That was my last joint you threw away. I can't score again till Bruce gives me some more money.'

10   Happy—Honest

HAPPY: cheerful and content with life. This is Kate since Andy's last telephone call announced that he has a week's holiday and will be arriving next weekend. It's difficult to know whether her pleasure is greatest at the thought of seeing Andy again or at the prospect of going home and rescuing the children from their self-directed existence. Mother is certain that it's far too soon for Kate to be going home to take care of the house and the whole brood again but Kate is determined to prove her wrong, and rushes about brightly sorting laundry and picking up cups and books and generally making a nuisance of herself to Joan. 'She is,' Mother darkly says, 'in danger of doing too much.'

The children are keen to see their father again and I don't think this has anything to do with the prospect of presents, though Julia does. But they are a little apprehensive, knowing that home means the end of a perfect holiday, to say nothing of a possible parting from Joey and the guinea-pigs. Kate is quite certain that Andy will be able to solve this problem.

Gabby is happy again, but doesn't visit us these days.

HARDY: something strong that can withstand ill winds.

HARPOON: a barbed spear fired by an explosive device, used for killing whales. The spear is attached to a long line which enables the whale to be retrieved and brought alongside the hunting vessel. Actually a single harpoon does not often kill a whale and many whales that have been hunted die slowly of harpoon wounds which must be to them like stab wounds to us. This is a very cruel practice. However, it is far from home and on the decline because of the danger of extinction for the whale. Something much more immediate and just as horrific seems to be the fate of crabs and lobsters, and they aren't offered protection by the threat of impending extinction.

Peter Potter catches these luckless creatures by luring them into wicker baskets on the sea bed, picking them up in his boat and taking them ashore. He is, of course, only one of many. So far they are still alive and kept in buckets of sea water, and cannot feel worse than a little peeved at being so roughly moved around and being deprived of their sand and seaweed. The real cruelty comes when someone throws them into a pan of boiling water, still alive. I'm assured by those who should know that nature has equipped these creatures with such sharp pincers and strong armour that there's no other way of dispatching them and thus bringing them to our tables. I find this very difficult to believe but have neither the courage nor the incentive to investigate the matter. It seems simpler just not to eat them.

I have come to be accused of being unreasonable about this, since we now have on hand a supply of cheap crab and lobster meat. Sebastian and Selena have taken to going out with Potter on his collecting trips and they return with the rewards of their labour. Or they did once. Nancy wasn't squeamish. She boiled up a big pot of water and then called Joan in to help her. Joan picked up a lobster and backed towards the stove, Nancy shut her eyes and lifted the lid and Joan reached out behind her and dropped the lobster into the water. The lid was firmly slammed back into place and they both stood with their hands over their ears to shut out the scream that came from the pan. Which is how I found them when I rushed into the kitchen to investigate the noise.

There was a second lobster awaiting its fate in a plastic bucket and it became very agitated, tipped over the bucket and made a sideways dash under the kitchen table. I believe it had been warned by the scream from the pot and was trying to make its escape but I'm told that this is impossible. Be that as it may, both Nancy and Joan dived beneath the table to catch the fugitive, which sent it hurtling towards me. I scooped it up again in the bucket and ran like hell across the garden, through the gate and the Forrester's garden and tipped the lobster into their creek. Sauntering back, swinging the bucket and trying to look nonchalant, I spied two faces peering curiously out of an upstairs window, Gabby's and Sven's. Joan and Nancy were very indignant that I'd removed half the ingredients of dinner but I assured them that it wouldn't be missed if I had anything to do with it.

'Now there's no call to be spoiling everyone else's pleasure,' Nancy said.

'How can you turn up your nose at a cheap meal when there's millions starving?' asked Joan. I could have seen the logic in her argument if we'd been short of money, or she had been trying to feed any of the starving millions. As it was I left them without discussing it further and went back to my work.

When the meal was ready I just helped myself to the salad and potatoes and said nothing. That would have been all if Mother hadn't said, 'Why aren't you having the lobster, Sally? It's quite fresh.'

'We caught it early this morning,' Sebastian said cheerfully.

'You may have caught it but I saw it die,' I said firmly.

Selena's glance at Sebastian told me that she had already raised this problem, and they too helped themselves only to vegetables.

Mother said, 'Really dear, you do make things difficult,' and took a large helping. Nancy, Joan and Jennifer also helped themselves, though I noticed that Jennifer took very little. Julia and Kate had welcomed a dish low in calories and already taken their share outside, so were unaffected. The meal continued in silence and gradually more and more of the white meat was pushed to the sides of the plates. No more lobsters appeared in the kitchen although Sebastian and Selena still went out on Potter's boat once or twice a week.

I wondered if it wasn't rather dangerous for Selena but Sebastian pointed out that since nobody could move far on a boat it actually put her at an advantage compared to her usual situation.

HARVEST: the gathering in of crops.

It's very easy to be preoccupied with the sea, living in this place, but only a short distance inland are many small mixed farms that have now begun to harvest cereals. I took the children along to watch the proceedings one afternoon and they stayed for a while, awestruck by the roar and clatter of machinery, but they decided that the tourist-strewn beach offered richer pickings in terms of entertainment and declined to repeat the excursion.

HAVEN: a safe and pleasant resting place. Our estuary is a haven for visiting sailing craft and when I notice the foreign flags they fly I can't help thinking that Peter Potter probably isn't the only smuggler in Cornwall. There is one particularly smart yacht, the *Rialto*, that has been anchored a little way out for some days now. Even I can see that it's beautiful and I know nothing about boats. The Commander sailed his little craft round and round it when it first appeared, like a bee worrying a bird. According to Selena, Potter says the owners are bankrupt and have to sell it. Nancy says this is true but the villagers think they're waiting for a chance to make a run for it to the Bahamas.

HAZE: a gentle mistiness in the air, that clouds the edge of the horizon in the evenings and promises the following day will be as sunny as the last. People keep saying the weather must break but we haven't had a drop of rain since we came here. The stream across the lawn has slowed to a trickle and won't wash the children any more. They think they make up for it by swimming daily in the sea. Their mother enticed them all indoors for hair washing yesterday and found a small dead fish clinging in the locks of Melly's hair. This caused a minor hysterical diverson.

HE: the male singular pronoun; as in 'he eats, he sleeps, he speaks, he knows.' He, he, he . . .

HEART: the organ of our bodies that pumps the blood around. Also, the part that has become falsely associated with emotions, particularly of loving and caring. The centre of emotion is really seated somewhere in the lower back portion of the brain, but this knowledge will not stop arrows through hearts being carved on trees or etched inside bus shelters with felt pens.

Nor will it stop people in Sven's situation declaring such things as, 'My heart is broken,' as he does every day by telegram to Julia. This caused the telephone operators first embarrassment then amusement as it was read out over the phone, but after four days they stopped phoning it through and simply send the confirmation copy with the morning post. Julia opens every one of the little yellow envelopes. 'After all, one day he might think of something original.'

HELICOPTER: a vertical take-off aircraft, kept in the air by one or more horizontal rotors.

I know I have said that the cottage garden is large but it's not all that large, and I thought Andy was taking a very great risk by landing that brand-new helicopter on the lawn. The unexpected stream very nearly caused him total disaster, and the wind from the rotor blew all the nappies off the clothes line. It was a pity that the people who would have been most impressed, the three

112

children, were on an expedition to the far side of the estuary in the Commander's dinghy. Little Stevie was terrified of the noise and ran into the house to be comforted by Jennifer. As Andy jumped out, flushed with pride and excitement, Kate advanced towards him with the baby held like a weapon and cried in dismay, 'You don't expect us to go home in that thing, do you?'

'Oh no, no, no!' he exclaimed jovially as he put an arm around her and steered her back towards the cottage. 'In fact I'm not supposed to be here at all but I just thought I'd give you all a surprise. I only got my licence to fly it last week.'

'I didn't know you were learning,' Kate said crossly.

The helicopter was a new toy that Andy's company had provided for its travelling sales executives and Andy had been arranging an exhibition in North Cornwall. He had thought it a good opportunity to see us all.

'But you'll see us next weekend, or had you forgotten?'

'Not forgotten, my sweet, but there's been a change of plan. One of our fellows is ill so I've got to cover his appointments in Norway.'

Because everyone was sitting around drinking tea and eating cream cake Kate just blinked back her tears and smiled understandingly. Precisely an hour after landing, Andy looked openly at his watch and said, 'Must be off now or they'll send out a search party. Thanks for the tea. Lovely to see you looking so much better, darling. Pity I missed the children.'

'Do drop in again sometime,' murmured Mother as he gave her a farewell peck on the cheek. 'And give us a chance to pick up these tea things before you start that damned engine.'

HELP: to give assistance. Sebastian has built wooden ramps to the back door and up one side of the verandah steps so that Selena can get in and out by herself.

*   *   *

HIDEOUT: a place to hide in secret, as Potter did in the woods so he could find out who was setting the badger traps. For a person who is so cruel to lobsters and eels he shows an amazing amount of concern about the badgers. In fact I learned later that it wasn't so much the capturing of badgers that made him angry as the methods used to snare them. Dogs were sometimes caught in snares, and children might be in danger too if they trespassed; and how are small children to know that wandering in woods on the cliff top is trespassing? Dogs certainly don't know. Anyway, after dismantling and destroying several snares, trespassing himself I suppose, Potter decided to keep a lookout and finally saw someone at work setting them up. He took it upon himself to punch the man on the nose but unfortunately it was the brother of the farmer who owned the cottage he lived in.

The fire in the thatch of Potter's cottage the next day provided spectacular entertainment for the tourists and in this very dry weather could easily have been started by a lighted cigarette being thrown onto the roof. It certainly began from the outside, soon after the pub had closed for the afternoon, and several people had heard the farmer promising death and destruction to Potter. The only person in the cottage at the time was Miranda, who was minding the shop and making more souvenirs, and she was quickly removed by a passer-by. Because it was daytime the blaze was soon spotted but by the time the fire brigade arrived there was no roof left and they completed the destruction by flooding the inside.

I relate all this because it left Potter with very few possessions and nowhere to live. It was Sebastian's suggestion that we should set up a temporary bed for him in one of our outhouses until he got himself sorted out. I don't know what 'sorted out' was supposed to mean because there was certainly no other accommodation in the village and as Potter's livelihood lay in the boat and the lobster pots he obviously wasn't going anywhere else in a hurry. If I'd been the one Sebastian asked I would have said he should sleep in the boat, but he asked Mother and she agreed that it would be all right. Kate was furious and Julia couldn't believe her luck.

Potter made the little outhouse passably comfortable in a temporary sort of way with a few boxes and one or two possessions he'd salvaged from his cottage. But at first he didn't sleep there. The window of Julia's room was just above the roof of the outhouse so he didn't even have to take the risk of walking through the house.

I knew about this because Julia's room was next to mine and although the outside walls of the cottage were thick, some of the internal ones were just partitions through which quite a lot could be heard. I must say I had to admire Julia for still being able to give so much of herself with her foot in plaster.

HITCH: something being held up: for instance hitching up a garment; hitching a lift by stopping a vehicle; a hold up in some plans.

The first major hitch in our domestic arrangements came about after Potter moved in, when Joan and Nancy put their collective respectable feet down. It was Mother they approached, as a pair, after breakfast. It had been the usual family breakfast: Mother and I reading letters or newspapers, Jennifer and Kate trying to persuade Stevie to eat an egg and passing cornflakes out of the window to the other children, the baby cooing in its carrycot in a corner of the room, Selena in her wheelchair, Julia reading yet another telegram, Sebastian in his running shorts after his early morning sprint around the village, and Potter wearing one of those sets of combination underwear that belong in old movies. It was understood that Potter could eat with us whenever he wanted because he was without means of cooking for himself, and he always wanted at breakfast time. His night-time activities didn't seem to take the edge off his appetite.

Joan and Nancy usually started on the washing up from this meal as soon as they arrived but on this day, after everyone except Mother, Julia and I had departed about their business, they ignored the debris and sat down at the table.

'We want to talk to you,' Nancy began.

'It's rather difficult,' continued Joan. Mother raised an eyebrow.

Just as I had expected, the work was too much for them. I wondered whether Mother would offer them more money or extra help.

'It's people,' said Nancy firmly. 'They're talking.'

'They do tend to,' I said. 'It's a design fault.'

'Please dear,' Joan pleaded, 'don't make things difficult.'

I didn't know I was. I listened.

'It all seemed so quiet and respectable at first but then it came to . . . to people on the dole . . .'

'And not married . . .'

'And carrying on . . .'

'And the kids running wild . . .'

'And then *him* . . .' They both glared at Julia.

'It's not just irregular any more, it's downright indecent.'

'Well, of all the . . .' muttered Julia.

Mother looked carefully at her nails. 'Are you suggesting that this household isn't good enough for you to earn your money in?'

'It's not that *we* mind,' Joan hurried on. 'Don't misunderstand. But my brother has a position to keep up in this village and . . .'

'Has he asked you to say this?'

'No, not exactly. But it has made things difficult with some of the people in the village.'

'Please don't be offended,' Nancy said quickly. 'It's not you we're on about.'

'I'm not offended,' Mother said with a smile. 'But I rather like my family and I'm sorry you find fault with

116

them. What are you thinking of doing about it?'

'We can't work here any more, that's flat.'

'And Jennifer?'

'That's the worst part of it, her sleeping in and so young too. Goodness knows what she's been seeing. She'll have to leave today.'

'And you two are leaving us in the lurch?'

'As soon as Jennifer's packed we'll be off,' Nancy said.

'Oh no dear, we'll do the washing up first,' said Joan.

'Well that's that then,' said Mother.

She kept calm while Julia and I were indignant at the very least. Then I realized that apart from Mother I was the only able-bodied person around who could manage the two smallest children and the meals. Indignation changed to a creeping anger, an inward kicking against the knowledge that there was no escape. I would *have* to do it; we wouldn't find anyone else in a hurry.

I went and told Kate what had happened and she said, 'I don't see that you've anything to complain about. You let your son bring that ruffian into the household. You should have told him to go instead of letting Mother lose her help.'

'But it's nothing to do with me. It's Mother and Sebastian, and Julia too.'

'How can you drag Julia into it?' Didn't she know? Oh yes, her bedroom was at the far end of the cottage—just so she could rest quietly, I remembered. 'You always try to shift the blame for your problems onto other people. I'll do what I can, of course, but you know I'm not really fit yet. Anyway, looking after the household is far more important than doing your silly thesis.'

Now where had I gone wrong? The way I understood it the purpose of living here at all this summer was to write my thesis. All other activities and members of the household were peripheral, theoretically anyway, though in practice I couldn't dismiss Mother or Sebastian as peripheral. Now that the periphery has taken over to

117

such an extent that I can no longer work, the object of our being here has disappeared, so we might as well pack up and go home.

HOBBLE: to walk in a crooked manner, usually because of deformation or injury to a foot or leg.

Julia's injury had recovered to the point where she could hobble on her plaster if necessary, but she preferred to languish in the sun or the shade, according to the time of day and the possible effect on her skin. On the morning when she received the telegram which said, 'Expect me at eleven for discussion about future,' she hobbled to her room and put on a very seductive silk dress, the effect of which was rather spoiled by the plaster. Then she settled herself in Kate's place on the hammock. At precisely eleven o'clock Sven came in through the front gate and strolled round to the lawn, dressed in impeccable pale blue trousers, a white silk shirt with a monogram on the pocket, and two-tone canvas shoes. He greeted us all with a courteous bow before he sat down, and Mother took the cue and fetched a tray of coffee with the best china cups. We sat and chatted over coffee though Julia was plainly wishing that we would go away and leave her to talk alone with Sven. I noticed a calm, relaxed, masterful air about him that had never been apparent before and which I think rather unnerved Julia. He really looked very attractive sitting there with his golden hair glinting, his tanned face aglow and his blue eyes twinkling assurance.

When the coffee was finished Kate and I took Mother's hint and began to collect the cups. But Sven stopped us.

'Just a minute, ladies, I'm sure you are all concerned in what I have come here to tell Julia. Do you mind, my dear?'

'How can I say if I don't know what it is? Go ahead. It's impossible to have a private row in this family anyway.'

'Row? I do not want a row. I just want to tell you that I have reached a decision. You may have your divorce.'

118

'Divorce?'

'Surely that is what you want?'

'I never said anything about a divorce.'

'But is that not the logical result of finishing things between us?'

Julia pouted and blinked her heavy eyelids.

'You see, my dear, I have been prepared to make many allowances because I wanted to keep you with me but now I have found someone else.'

'Why didn't you tell me before?'

'Before what? I couldn't tell you before I knew myself. I have only recently found this person.'

'Am I allowed to know who it is?'

I held my breath, anticipating the bombshell. 'But surely you know where I am staying? You know about Gabby?'

'Gabby? Is that who you mean? I thought you meant someone *else*!' Julia started to laugh.

'But isn't Gabby someone else enough? You must take it seriously. I have fallen in love. I will marry Mrs Forrester.'

HOBBY: an activity undertaken for pleasure in a person's spare time. There are many varied hobbies in our household alone: for instance Julia's association with Potter could have been described as a hobby, though it came to an abrupt end after Sven's strange visit. The nights were quiet again except for stifled sobs. The bed in the outhouse was slept in.

With children, who do not have to earn a living, it's sometimes hard to know where play ends and hobbies begin, but Roger and Miranda have certainly become engrossed in the intricacies of making shell souvenirs for tourists. Since Peter's stock was destroyed in the fire they've missed their commission on sales and so they've started up a little workshop of their own in the summer-house under Potter's supervision. As they're making a financial profit I suppose it isn't strictly a hobby but they gain immense pleasure from it.

Sebastian's hobby of running has become more frequent and obsessive and it's worried me slightly because it's so uncharacteristic of the Sebastian I knew. Selena's only comment has been, 'He has to use up the energy. He's hyperactive. It's a side effect of the treatment.' What treatment? She didn't go on to tell me and I felt afraid to ask.

Selena's cooking has come in very useful. As soon as Nancy departed she took over the kitchen: all the cooking, cleaning and washing. At first we all rushed to help but she is so quietly firm about wanting to do it on her own and is obviously quite capable of coping. 'It's my contribution,' she said. While she's busy doing all that, Sebastian cleans the cottage almost as often and quite as effectively as Joan ever did, as well as doing the garden. They also manage, between them, to look after Stevie and the baby some of the time, though Kate has more or less taken over again there.

Nobody asked them to do all these things and they never actually volunteered. It just sort of dawned on me that it was happening. With Mother as overseer and manager the household works perfectly without me having to do more than a bit of washing up.

HONEST: saying what you really think; behaving in accordance with your principles and ideals.

Most people are not strictly honest with themselves or those around them and people who are honest often make things difficult for themselves. The trouble is it's hard to know whether a person is being honest or not. Take Julia, for instance, tying herself and Sven up in knots, to say nothing of Potter and Gabby and the Commander, and nobody really knows what she wants. I wonder if she does herself.

And what about Mother? I asked her if she'd meant what she said about liking her family. That had surprised me. She has so often given the impression of disapproving.

'Of course I like you all.'

'The way we are? Really?'

She sighed. 'I know I did try to make you into different kinds of people. That's what you're getting at, isn't it? I meant you all to turn into respectable wives and mothers. But somehow Kate's the one I worry about most. She's so put upon and doesn't realize it. But how can I not be proud of Julia's beauty and your independence and Sebastian's honesty?'

'Sebastian's honesty?' Now that one just hadn't struck me. Devious and underhand was more the way I'd have put it.

'Yes of course. Look at the way he contributes to the household.'

'I presume he does the work because he likes it.'

'He likes the gardening. I think he does the housework to save you or me having to do it.'

I must say I hadn't considered it as carefully as she obviously had. 'You think that's honesty?'

'Well, I'd class it rather more as nobility. He showed his honesty best the day he arrived and asked to be put in the same room as Selena. Most young men would have been a bit circumspect in a household ruled by a grand-mother, wouldn't they?'

'Yes, but I suppose he knew you'd understand it was just so that he could look after her.'

'Is that what you believe about them, Sally?'

'How could it be anything else? Selena's paralysed from the waist down, isn't she?'

'I know she can't move her legs but that doesn't say anything about her feelings, does it? All I do know is that they pushed the two single beds together the day after they arrived. Haven't you been into their room?'

I shook my head. I just hadn't considered it that way at all. He'd never wanted to cuddle me, why should he want physical contact with anyone else? He'd never liked girls, had he? I'd assumed that attaching himself to a cripple was a way in which he could evade the issue.

'He's never told me how he feels. I'd hoped he might want to talk to me after he came back, but he hasn't tried at all.'

'Have you?'

'Have I what?'

'Tried to talk to him?'

'Well, no, I mean, wouldn't it be an intrusion? Like being nosey?'

'Perhaps he can't make the first move, Sally. You are his mother and without a father around you have always been the only disapproving adult in his life. He hasn't had anyone else to turn to when he thinks he's failed you.'

Except Bruce, and I sent Bruce away.

'Mother, where did you learn all this psychology?'

'It's not psychology, it's common sense. Perhaps that's why you need it explaining to you.'

11   I—Intention

I: the first person singular pronoun, which this is all
about, but I fear just another delusion really. I would like
to be a singular person as much as anyone else but there
must be many more people just like me, which doesn't
make me singular at all. I know there are other people
who look like me because of the number of times a complete stranger comes rushing up to me exclaiming, 'Jane
(or Mary or Jackie or Sharon)! Fancy seeing you here!'
Or something like that. It happened to me on the beach
yesterday. This male person leaps towards me scatter-
ing sand in people's faces and cries, 'Pam! After all this
time!'

'No, it's not.' I step back hurriedly to avoid being
swept into an embrace that might permanently disfigure
me and make it impossible to regain my own identity.

'Not what?' he asks stupidly, eyes still shining.

'I'm not Pam. I'm Sally.'

'Oh my God! I'm so sorry! Of course I can see now . . .'
And he droops away not even game to press home his
advantage. I am obviously no substitute for Pam even if I
do look like her.

It has occurred to me now that I begin the Is that I must
take a stand about words beginning with 'im' or 'in' that
are merely the negative of the words without the prefix.
I will not define any of these words, if I can help it. I add
the safeguard of 'if I can help it' because I can see
already as I churn words through my brain that by no

means all of the words beginning with 'im' or 'in' are negative words so some of the wrong kind may just slip in without my noticing.

Another odd thing is worth mentioning. Many of these words have a perfectly recognizable positive without the prefix but quite a lot of them, whilst recognizably negative words, do not readily convert to a positive term in everyday use. For instance, take words like impatient, immoral, inaccurate, incapable. We can just as easily use the positives of these, but take words like impeccable, inept, intransigent. I should be able to say the following:

'Potter's clothes were peccable at all times.'

'We were surprised to find that Selena was so ept a cook.'

There are also such words beginning with 'dis'. Am I gruntled when things are going well? Do I parage people when they please me? But thereby must hang someone else's story.

I really am getting well on with my thesis now. In spite of the fact that Pope thought I wouldn't have enough original material for a PhD, it's coming along very nicely and I'm having less time to do my Bruce Wild, though I go back to it from time to time because I can't really say my mind is at rest about Sebastian. I find myself brooding on too many unanswered questions. Is he really cured of the drug habit? What'll he do when we leave here? What about Selena?

I haven't let Pope know that Sebatian has turned up but yesterday I got a postcard from him in Brittany reminding me that he wanted to know, just in case I might be able to forget, I suppose. I stuck it on the mantelpiece in the sitting room alongside the exotic postcards from Mother's many friends. This morning I found Sebastian looking at it, in the course of polishing the ornaments and horse brasses that surround the fireplace. 'Are you going to tell him?' he asked as he

124

replaced the card and continued with his polishing.

'That's up to you to do if you want to. But you did make him very angry by sending him your Bruce Wild. Why did you do that?'

Sebastian carefully smeared polish onto the surface of the metal before answering. 'It seemed to have quite a lot to do with him.' Rub rub.

'He said it was obscene.'

'Critical, Mum, critical.' Rub rub, breathe on it, rub again.

'He said he wouldn't want Paula to see it.'

'I didn't send it to Paula.'

'He didn't want me to read it either.'

'You don't need to. You already know what a rotten bugger he is.'

'Not entirely. He's a very clever man.'

'Mum, is there supposed to be a logical connection there?' He stopped polishing and looked up. His face was flushed and defensive. I was afraid of probing too far, too fast.

'Why do you go to all the trouble of cleaning these ornaments? Nobody cares.'

'Gran does. I do. The people who put them here do. They look beautiful when they're finished. I wrote about how it makes me sick every time I've thought of him pawing and fucking you and I'd rather not be alive than know it happened.' The words came out very quickly and were followed by a furious bout of repolishing the pieces he had already done.

'It was all right at the time, really it was. He was pretty nice in those days.'

Sebastian shook his head, calm again. 'No, you only thought he was, like you thought Bruce was okay.'

'But if I think so, then it is so for me, surely?'

'Not really. It's only okay if it goes on feeling right afterwards. Otherwise you got it wrong. It's not easy. Bruce had me fooled too. People are very hard to get the hang of.'

*   *   *

125

IAMBIC: a kind of regular limping rhythm used in poetry, in the days when poetry needed to have rhythm about it. Modern poetry gets along without rhythm but is strong on meaning. I used to be quite good at writing and analysing poetry at school but I went off it a bit in the sixth form when the teacher told me my efforts lacked sensitivity.

IBID: if you come across this in the footnotes of a book or article you are reading it means refer to the reference that has already been specified. It would also mean that you are reading very learned stuff, which other people tend to resent if you've said you find it interesting and they can't understand it.

ICARUS: this was the foolish fellow who made wings of wax, which were quite successful until he became so pleased with himself that he flew too near the sun. Yes, you remember, the wings melted and he fell into the sea and was drowned.

ICE: frozen water, very cold.
   The ice in our lives at the moment is either clinking around in glasses, or ice cream which seems to reach us in big plastic tubs which are kept in the freezer.

IDIOT: a person with no intelligence, very stupid. One can have quite a lot of intelligence and still behave like an idiot if one is not applying one's intelligence to the situation in hand. Like me with Bruce, for instance.
   I was naturally rather upset to discover that Sebastian was buying hash with money that Bruce handed out to him unknown and unapproved by me. Interfering in my financial arrangements with my son was on the same level as telling him secrets about his parentage, and I'd never got over that particular surge of anger, though I'd learned to live with it. At the point of finding out about the money, I left Sebastian to his own

dozey devices and went to do things in the kitchen and somehow I began to cry.

To say that I don't often cry is an overstatement. Apart from tears coming into my eyes when I peel onions or stub my toe or whack my thumb with a hammer, this was the first time since that day so long ago when I'd been counselled by my friendly client. The upheaval of emotional sobs is an experience I can well do without. Especially as on this occasion it led to a bewildered Bruce putting his arms around me and trying to kiss away my tears. (Does he like the taste of salt? I remember asking myself at the time). This put me at a severe disadvantage for being aggressive and challenging. I tried though. I pushed him away and demanded to know why he'd been giving Sebastian the extra cash, and whether he knew what it was being used for.

'A friendly gesture. I was always short of money as a kid so when he says he needs it I feel sorry for him. I've got it. What he uses it for is his own business, isn't it?'

'Not the way I see it. Don't you understand about responsibility? Sebastian's past the age of sweets and comics. He's into smoking dope.'

'Yes, I know.'

'You know? And you still give him the means to do it?'

'If I didn't he'd find it elsewhere, by worse means.'

'But you're making it easy for him. You're encouraging him to think it's all right.'

'He's never needed my encouragement. He found out all about it at that school of his before I came on the scene. But he has talked to me about it.'

'Why you and not me?'

'You're his keeper, I'm his friend.'

It was true. But why couldn't I be both? I had stopped crying and Bruce had a comforting arm around my shoulders. Society has got it right, really. Kids need two people, one to fight against and one to confess to. One person can't be both. I felt relief that I didn't have to take a moral stand and tell Bruce to move out.

'Can't you use your friendship to try to stop him?' I wanted to know.

'I do try. But if I take the heavy parent role it'll do no good at all. He doesn't do it all the time, you know. He gets depressed sometimes and then breaks out. You know, some of the money I gave him was spent on that birthday present he gave you.'

'The briefcase?' I'd wondered how he'd afforded it, even suspected him of coming by it dishonestly.

After that we were all more open with each other, or so I thought. We discussed and made a regular arrangement about Sebastian's access to finance and Bruce became more like a full member of the family than a permanent lodger. I steered clear of implying a lack of trust by constantly asking questions about the drug situation and Sebastian became more cheerful and sociable, and even seemed to spend time doing his homework.

I was grateful to Bruce. I loved him. Either from that new feeling of a shared problem, or from some addictive quality in cuddling and kissing away tears, sex between us became altogether softer and more caring. We began to do it quite a lot; for a few months it really was the most interesting side of our life.

Yes, I was an idiot.

IDLE: a person or machine not working.

Now that Kate is on her feet much of the time, that applies to nobody in our household except Julia, whose leg is still in plaster. She's due to have it taken off (the plaster not the leg) in a couple of days' time. I expect she'll need some physiotherapy after that but I don't suppose she'll go climbing the cliffs again. She's spent most of her time in her room this week and she looks very pale and tired, not her usual confident self. I know Mother takes her little tasty titbits of food on a tray and tries to talk to her. I rather think she's hoping that Sven will be overcome with remorse when he realizes what

128

he's done to her and will come to her bedside begging forgiveness. That's the way they do it in films.

I think Sven is still interested in Julia because I catch the glint of sunlight on his field-glasses from time to time. There's a spot on the hillside about half a mile away which gives him a superb view onto our terrace. It must also enable him to see into Julia's bedroom window if she hasn't drawn the blind. Also, there hasn't been the kind of disturbance between the Forresters that would indicate that a divorce has been proposed. I don't think Sven has actually mentioned to Gabby that he wants to marry her. I think that Gabby would throw him out if she thought he'd become serious because Gabby likes her life as it is and is really very fond of her husband. I expect Sven knows this.

IMAGE: a reflection or likeness, or a conceptual viewpoint held in the mind. For instance, we hold images of the people around us which do not necessarily conform to the reality of what those people are like. It is suggested that people really are what we believe them to be but I would dispute that theory. It could lead to the uncomfortable conclusion that none of us exists at all except in each other's minds.

Mother's image in the Commander's eyes underwent a change on the day of the speedboat ride. The first I knew about it was the sound of a high-powered engine and then the sight of a small boat tearing along the estuary. I was enjoying an afternoon stroll along the overlooking hillside, accompanied by Joey who had not been allowed to be included in the day's activities by the younger members of the family, and I could see all the sailing craft trying to avoid being swamped by the speedboat's wake. It circled the anchored yacht and shot across to the far side of the estuary. I could imagine the cursing and swearing going on down below and I smiled with the superior air of one who is not merely an ignorant holiday maker. A figure loomed up by my side and pushed a pair of field-glasses into my hands. I wasn't surprised to see Sven; I had caught sight of his hat in the bracken about a quarter of an hour before. Gabby was with him, wearing jeans and a fluffy shirt that was covered with specks of grass and bracken. I wondered if they knew about adders. I think Gabby was a little hesitant about me seeing them together; after all, I was a confidante of the Commander on occasions, but Sven was quite agitated about the speedboat and not at all concerned about security risks.

'Take a look!' he muttered. 'Take a look! I don't believe it!'

'They are behaving badly,' I agreed. The craft was now quite close to our side of the estuary. I had difficulty at first in sorting out my field of vision but while they were heading straight towards us for a few moments I found it easier to focus. I didn't believe it either. There were four people in the boat: Potter, Sebastian, Selena and Mother. Selena and Sebastian sat in the back seat and in the front Potter had one arm around Mother who was at the wheel. She was laughing with a crazed abandon.

I knew they'd set off together in the car but I thought they were shopping. Instead it seemed they'd gone mad. I passed the field-glasses to Gabby who now stood beside me. She watched while the boat swung round in a wide curve and headed back up the river. Then she trained the glasses on the dinghy with the red sails, wallowing in the outwash. A little smile played on her face. 'I like your mother,' she said.

INDIGNANT: righteously angry.

Of course the Commander was indignant and actually came round to complain that evening rather than making a social call. We managed to persuade him to accept a gin and he strode up and down the room lecturing us, pointing his finger and clinking the ice about in his glass.

'You really are a totally irresponsible family! You come here under the guise of studious respectability and you collect around you a crowd of layabouts and drop-outs, you steal water from the village stream—and believe me there'll be questions raised about that at the next Parish Council meeting—and as a last straw you try to sink half the sailors on the estuary.'

'We were only having a bit of fun,' Sebastian protested. But the Commander was deeply suspicious of Sebastian and not prepared to see him as an innocent.

'You've led your poor grandmother into enough trouble already, young man. Do you have to terrify her half out of her wits by a silly trick like that? My dear Mrs Fry, don't you think you'd better come and live with me while Sally gets this lot sorted out?'

We were all watching him with interest, nobody wanting to be the first to interrupt. But at that point Mother fixed him with a direct stare and asked, 'Are you making an improper suggestion, Commander?'

He stopped in mid-stride. 'Oh no, my dear, as though I would! Merely meant to offer you my protection.'

'It's been done before,' muttered Sebastian. 'Dirty old man.'

'Now really, please keep out of this.' Commander Forrester was blushing. 'Your generation may think that anything goes but I wouldn't dream of making any proposition to a lady unless I was a free man.'

'Well you soon may be,' Julia said with some venom. 'Why don't you try him out for size, Mother? He looks a nice fatherly figure.'

He looked around the room from one to another, suddenly unsure of himself. 'Why don't you have another drink?' I asked. On every face a smile lurked but this time we had gone too far. He wasn't prepared to laugh at the situation.

'No thank you,' he replied. 'I don't think I will.' He placed his glass carefully on a table and stalked out of the room.

INTENTION: what a person believes will be done or achieved in the future. It is Andy's stated intention to

131

drive down next week to collect Kate and the children. I mention this because I don't really think he will, but Kate's faith is such that she has already started packing odds and ends.

It is my intention to talk to Sebastian more and to try to see Sven alone and straighten things out there before any more damage is done. I will benefit from the first but not from the second, and nobody may thank me for either.

I also intend to finish my thesis before I go back to London even if nobody understands why. Kate did apologize and explain that she doesn't really think it's silly but she can't think why I waste my time on it. 'After all, it's your holiday. Your own free time. You're not getting paid for it.'

'I like doing it.'

'All that time closeted in your room in this lovely weather? You like it? I think it's just because you're so lonely, Sally. It's a defence mechanism, you know. What you really need is to find yourself a nice man.'

12   Jabber—Jungle

'Hey, Mum, you're doing one too!'

I came into my room to find Sebastian, duster in hand, peering at the papers on my desk. 'How's it going?'

'I find it very easy to assemble, if that's what you mean. How did yours go? Did you send it all to Pope?'

'Most of it. It only came in bits and pieces, then when I got to F for Father I began to get better.'

'How did you know you were getting better?'

'I could go a whole day without needing to see the therapist.' He tucked the duster into his belt and sat down in the armchair, his eyes shining. 'It was wonderful, Mum, you've no idea!'

'What therapist is this? You forget, I still don't know where you've been.'

'You do really. You remember all those places you took me to see when you wanted me cured and I didn't? You remember the place where they hypnotized people every time they wanted to go back on their drugs? That's where I went. Well, it seemed so nice and gentle; nobody crying in corners or dragging themselves around.'

'But why didn't you tell me? Why leave me wondering for three months?'

'I know that wasn't good but I didn't care then. It mightn't have worked and then I was as good as dead anyway. I wasn't too crazy to understand that.'

'And you're cured now?'

'You can see for yourself. I've got Selena. If I relapse she sets off the trigger to hynotize me again and I do the same for her.'

133

'Is that all there is to it?'

'That, and keeping busy. Always knowing what's the next thing to be done.'

It began to make sense. 'But what happens if you lose Selena? What if she goes away?'

'It's the same for her. We can't leave each other.'

'How did you find her?'

'I didn't. We were given to each other. Selena started on drugs after her accident. She couldn't cope with the wheelchair and the pain. Neither of us was in a fit state to choose when they paired us off. I was lucky, wasn't I?'

JABBER: to talk quickly and continuously without making much sense.

Little Stevie's conversation is mostly jabbering. The poor little fellow has really had the worst deal of anybody this summer. He badly wants his older brothers and sisters to play with him and quite often sets off in pursuit of them when he hears their voices in the distance. But he simply isn't allowed to leave the garden although he often tries to make his escape, even aided and abetted on occasions by Melly who thinks it's just too hard-hearted to go off and leave him behind on his own. He comforts himself by talking to the guinea-pigs, and when Sebastian made a larger pen for them so they could run on the lawn during the day Stevie actually managed to climb inside with them, much to Kate's disgust.

He's very fond of his little baby brother, who's far too young to be of any use as a playmate, but when the baby's awake Stevie talks to him, too, and devotes a lot of ingenuity to bringing him interesting things to amuse him, like flowers and toy trucks and Lego bricks. The height of his inspiration came when he gave the guinea-pigs to the baby to play with, or perhaps he meant it to be the other way round. I could see the perfect logic in his mind of introducing his favourite companions to each other and he was very puzzled when this didn't meet with adult approval. In fact Kate went so far as to smack him soundly for it and his little tear-stained face as he plodded disconsolately around the lawn reminded me of Sebastian when I had punished him, also probably unfairly it seems now. Oh Sebastian, if only I could have you back again, do it all over again without the bad bits that could have been avoided! Will Kate think the same one day, when it's too late?

The baby wasn't harmed by the guinea-pigs but they only escaped with their lives then because Kate couldn't find anyone who was willing to undertake execution. Even Potter took their side. Mother suggested putting up a notice in the minimarket to see if new owners could be found.

JAM: a conserve of preserved fruits, sweet and sticky, for spreading on bread and toast on dark winter days, and also from time to time on faces, chairs and into hair and sleeping bags, and oh what a to-do there was when Kate decided she felt well enough to start sorting out the camp with a view to packing that up too. She did get them into clean beds but then they decamped to the verandah in the middle of the night and that compromise continued, mainly because there was no way of stopping it. Locking the doors resulted in them climbing out of the windows and even Kate wasn't willing to stay up all night to mount guard.

JEALOUSY: a state of envy or suspicion of someone who has something that you want for yourself. I'm told that jealousy can be an even more overwhelming emotion than love. The only time I can remember experiencing it was when Bruce showed me the neatly-bound volume of his PhD and the awarding letter from the University. I thought at first that I was just irritated because I'd been washing his shirts and cooking his meals while he'd spent all his spare time writing it up, but as the feeling persisted and grew I thought, why him and not me? He had made himself superior at my expense. I could have done what he'd done, but not at the same time as nurturing him.

JELLY: a transparent food preparation, soft but stiff due to the presence of gelatin which is made from bones. Jelly can be sweet or savoury, according to taste. A great deal of the sweet variety went the same way as the jam.

JILT: to break up with a lover.

There has been a lot of jilting since Julia arrived. She jilted Sven, then Potter jilted Gabby, then Sven jilted her, then she jilted Potter. The next move seems to be either Gabby jilting the Commander, or Sven jilting Gabby, either of which could cause problems, or Gabby jilting Sven which might even things up.

Julia is still pining away in her room and only emerging at sunset when the ice begins to clink in the glasses. Her excuse is that her ankle is very stiff since the plaster was taken off but it must be getting better because Selena massages it for her two or three times a day. It's quite true that she is very upset, though it's uncertain whether this is because Sven wants to leave her, because he wants to leave her for Gabby in particular, or because he made the announcement in such a public way.

JOY: a kind of intense happiness, usually given extrovert expression.

Joy aptly describes the result of my feelings for Bruce during that happy year when Sebastian stopped smoking dope and began to work for his 'O' levels and Bruce was engaged on his thesis. The jealousy came later. It was the joy that enabled me to wash his socks and cope with all the shopping and cooking without questioning why I was doing it. I suppose I did quite well to maintain this state of mind for a whole year but some people manage it for far longer and in a way it would have been better if I'd never come to my senses. The first creeping doubts brought on by my envy of Bruce's achievement were followed by a terrible sense of insecurity when he began applying for posts in other parts of the country without, apparently, giving any thought to my interest in the matter.

JUDGE: to make distinctions of quality or of right and wrong between competing objects or factions.

Quite early on in the summer Mother had been asked to judge the cake-baking competition at the Cricket Club fête. In spite of the ill feeling towards us from some quarters in the village, the club secretary was still keen to have her services and even rang up to remind her of it a few days beforehand. Mother was determined to make a good job of it and Selena spent some time coaching her about the proper qualities of a 'good' cake, and baking examples for her to try.

JUNGLE: a rain forest with very thick undergrowth, the sort of environment where the first guerilla warfare used to take place.

I decided that the only way to get to talk to Sven was to play anti-guerillas and was thankful that the terrain around us only offered bracken and a few small thickets rather than real jungle.

I pinpointed Sven's favourite spot overlooking the cottage and after lunch I climbed up the hillside and hid myself on top of a little outcrop of rocks near the top. I knew that Sven wouldn't have Gabby with him that afternoon because there was a mid-week cricket match and she always gave the game priority over other distractions. The hilltop was pretty quiet. One group of walkers tramped past but most seaside holiday-makers only go for walks when it rains and this afternoon, as any other, activity was centred at the water's edge. From where I was I could look down at the estuary watching the little boats like toys on the water. The larger boats looked more stately and superior. The yacht *Rialto* was still moored a little way out; it had shown no sign of life since it had arrived. Insects bumbled and whirred around me in a warm sort of way and presently I heard the repeated clack of the cricket match echoing up from the village.

I was woken by a wet snuffling in my face and I couldn't at once collect my senses to think where I was, let alone who might be molesting me. The snuffle was repeated, more insistently, and I rolled away and lashed out a hand that came into contact with Joey's shaggy coat. Then I heard a little giggle, quickly stifled by 'Shhh . . .' and I saw the grinning faces of Miranda, Rog and Melly peering over the rocks. They signalled urgently to me to be quiet as well and I held onto Joey, sat up and looked where they were pointing. I could see Sven's hat in the bracken about fifty yards downhill from us.

'What's going on,' I whispered.

The children crowded into my hollow with me, still whispering. 'We're stalking Uncle Sven.'

'Yes, I can see that. Why?'

'We often do. He does the most interesting things. Haven't you noticed?'

'Well, a little.'

'You see, we pretend he's a revenue man and we're the smugglers' look-outs.'

'Or he's a spy and we're the army.'

'Does he know?'

'Of course not. That would spoil the fun.'

'Sometimes he gets away though.'

'But today he's dead.'

'He's been shot. Just before Joey found you.'

I started, realizing that the hat hadn't moved at all while I'd been watching. 'Dead? Really?'

'Oh, you are silly. No, of course not really. It's pretend.'

'I tell you what,' I suggested. 'Suppose you pretend

you only wounded him and now you have to take him prisoner and bring him to me for interrogation.'

Eyes shone. 'Really Sally? Oh, what fun!'

'Great idea.'

'Okay.' Miranda took command. 'Rog, you go to the right, Melly to the left and I'll stay behind him and cut off his retreat. Circle round before you show yourselves.'

I kept Joey with me and the operation was carried out with a precision that the Royal Marines would have been proud of. Less than ten minutes later a red faced and embarrassed Sven was escorted up the hill, a little canvas belt pulled tight around each wrist in lieu of handcuffs. 'Here he is, Captain,' Roger announced as he hauled Sven over the rocks. 'Shall we get him ready for torture?'

Sven didn't know whether to be angry or relieved when he saw me. I suppose he thought I had organized the whole thing but at least my presence meant that there wouldn't be any real torture—possibly. The children made him give his word that he wouldn't escape before they released his hands, just in time to prevent Melly from losing her trousers altogether.

'Right,' said Roger, focussing on the very same opening question that was in my mind. 'What are you doing spying on our headquarters?'

'Headquarters? Well, I was trying to determine the strength of the enemy.' He smiled nervously, still unsure of whether this was truly a game or for real.

'Why? Are you going to launch an attack?'

'Something like that.'

'Not by himself he isn't,' muttered Miranda. 'Confess now, who are you working for?'

'Oh, I work for myself.'

'Liar! Liar!' Joey added fierce barks here as he always did to reinforce the children when they raised their voices. 'What's the point of gathering information if you work for yourself?'

'Why, that's easy. I sell to the highest bidder.'

139

'A mercenary! What shall we do with him?'

'Find someone who'll buy him,' suggested Melly with commendable practicality.

'Who?'

'The Commander might.'

'But he's playing cricket.'

'We could keep him prisoner until the tea break but that's ages and it means we can't go anywhere else.' This was too much of a problem.

'Oh, I don't care!' moaned Miranda, sprawling against the rock. 'It's too hot for war. Let's go swimming.'

'We haven't time. We've got to meet Potter's boat at four o'clock.'

'We can swim near the jetty while we wait for the boat.'

'That means wearing costumes. We'll have to go home first and then Mummy'll catch us and make us have tea.'

This prospect filled them with gloom for a moment, then Melly suggested, 'Why don't we swim in our knickers then just put our trousers on top again.'

'Oh yes, good idea. Are you coming Sally, Uncle Sven?'

'No,' I said quickly. 'We want to talk a bit longer. You go, and be careful.'

'We always are.' I watched their heads and shoulders ploughing through the bracken; at least, two heads and shoulders, followed by Melly's head only, and the tip of Joey's tail. I hadn't wanted to insult them by sending them off to buy ice creams but I had been wondering how I could get Sven to myself.

'Now then, Sven,' I began severely. 'Why *are* you spying on headquarters?'

'I want to see what Julia is doing.'

'But what's the point if you're not interested in her any more?'

'Did I say I was not interested?'

'You said you wanted to divorce her.'

'Ah Sally, I hadn't suspected you of having an illogical

mind. To say I want a divorce is not to say I am not interested.'

Rattled, I looked at him more closely. I have to admit that I had never really had any opportunity to get to know Sven. I'd met him at the wedding and at occasional family gatherings since. Most of my assumptions about him had come through Julia and most of the time she gave the impression that he was a bit of a clown. His eccentric Englishman get-up rather added to this. But it just wasn't consistent with the public image of a film maker of some repute who had won prizes and made quite a lot of money for himself. As I looked at those twinkling blue eyes it occurred to me that there might be quite a lot of play acting going on here.

'You've made Julia very unhappy,' I said, starting from another tack.

He nodded. 'It was intentional. It will make her think.'

'She's certainly doing that. She's thinking very angry thoughts about you for making a fool of her.'

'Well, she has not always worried about my dignity.'

'You mean sleeping with Potter? She's stopped that.'

'I know. But he is nothing. You must be aware that your sister is a very naughty woman. She prefers to sleep with almost any man but me. A smelly old fisherman is no surprise.'

'Perhaps she's disappointed in marriage.'

'Of course she is. But she knew before we married that I was more interested in art than sex. I work so hard that I am too tired for sex, except when I have a holiday. Then she complains not only that she gets too little but that what she gets is not good enough. Now how does she know it's not good enough, I ask myself, if she is not constantly making comparisons? So then I feel guilty that I'm letting her down and that makes things worse. Now this little holiday has given me time and Gabby has shown me that there is nothing wrong with me at all, only what Julia has put into my mind.'

'Yes, that's another point,' I interrupted, not wanting

141

to hear any more about his sexual problems. Sven's reticence was physical rather than verbal. 'What about Gabby Forrester? Have you really asked her to marry you?'

'Oh no!' He laughed outright. 'I know she plays games with me. If she thinks I am serious she will put me out. She is very happy with her totally reasonable sailor. And if Julia is now jealous then I have it both ways, yes?'

'But what about the Commander?'

Sven shrugged. 'We are very discreet, very careful. You are worried about the Commander's feelings?'

'Mother is. We're in enough trouble already.'

'Oh yes, the speedboat, your Sebastian. Very funny. Now then, it is nearly time for me to put the supper in the oven.'

'You?'

'Yes, on cricket days I have to do this. My terms for board and lodging are "en famille" you know.' Very much so.

'And are you going to carry on spying on Julia?'

'Perhaps I had better find another look-out position, don't you think? I don't want to be captured again.'

As we walked down the hill he asked, 'Do you think Julia wants me back because she cares for me or because she doesn't want Gabby to have me?'

This rang a bell as the sort of question I used to discuss eagerly with my friends on the way home from school. All part of the Great Illusion as to the Importance of Romance. Not the sort of question I expected from an adult man, though.

'Does it matter? Surely the important thing is to know whether you want her or not.'

13   Kaaba—Knit

I could say quite a lot about KAABA, which is the sacred
shrine of the Moslems, or KABUL, the capital city of
Afghanistan, or KAFFIRS, who live somewhere in the
third world, and you would be surprised at how far I
could get before I had to stop and look things up. If I was
really on that desert island I would do all that because
sacred black stones or Himalayan cities would seem just
as interesting and relevant to my life as Mother and the
family do now. But at the moment they don't have the
same immediacy. Perhaps, though, I'm cheating,
because I'm not doing a Bruce Wild under instruction
from a therapist. I mean, I know the relevance of everything I write as soon as it comes into my mind, before it
hits the paper, so to speak. I know as much about it as
Bruce does, which is more than anyone else in the world,
even the people who are now climbing onto the band-
wagon and 'criticizing' or 'improving' his work. Apart
from being in on the conception I read the finished
article very carefully when it had dawned on me that I
must aim to compete.

The basic principle of the Bruce Wild Therapy is that
when the subject has completed each day's writing, or
talking into a tape recorder, the therapist analyses it by
scoring a point for every time mention is made of a particular person, place or incident in the subject's life.
Gradually a graph is built up and you can see a pattern
of the most important features that have unconsciously
come to the surface. For many people this is quite

predictable, as with the mother who goes on about nothing but babies, the teenager who can only sensibly discuss the latest pop group, or the teacher whose discourse continually returns to schools. But some people's principal concerns are totally submerged, a form of defence mechanism because they're so painful, and they are the people who have problems. If you get hold of a copy of Bruce's book you'll see how neatly these problems emerge by using the therapy and how as soon as people become aware of their areas of difficulty and get over being surprised by them, they begin to talk about it and find solutions to their own problems. Now, Sebastian stopping at FATHER because he made one meaningful response isn't really doing the thing properly. Bruce would say there might be other problems that are still hidden and I imagine that if he'd let himself get onto FOOD he might have got an even better insight. However good a sign it was that he began to shake off his addiction, I do believe that Pope wasn't the only cause of his problems.

KALE: a kind of leafy green plant, quick growing, useful for both animal and human consumption. I believe that it is a close landlubbing relation of seaweed, which just shows that humans do not have the monopoly of problems with relations.

KANGAROO: an antipodean marsupial. Or in other words an animal from Australia who keeps its young in a pouch. This animal enjoys the amazing advantage of having a sort of delayed-action pregnancy. Even if fertilized, it doesn't gestate its young while it still carries one in the pouch. Imagine being able to get pregnant but put off actually producing the child until it was convenient! Now wouldn't that just change society? Another advantage for the kangaroo is that its baby when born is only an inch or two long which must be most undisturbing. We humans have not been altogether

144

clever about this evolution game. But who wants to look like a kangaroo?

KETTLE: originally a pot for boiling food in, now specifically used for boiling water. Which is why I had such problems with the concept of a 'pretty kettle of fish', a phrase which my father was fond of using on occasions. Now, how on earth would one get fish into a kettle? And why would they be there anyway? Small fish, like goldfish, might quite like it but we wouldn't be able to see them, and what would happen to them if we wanted to make a cup of tea? And anyway, what had that got to do with a broken bicycle or burnt toast?

I did sort that one out somewhere in the course of my education, probably from some dictionary. Have you noticed that's only the second time I've mentioned my father? I don't seem to have had any problems with him, but he was only a vague voice downstairs in the evenings most of the week and at weekends I seem to remember being constantly exhorted not to upset him. This seems strange because he was never upset about anything, just muttered, 'This is a pretty kettle of fish.' Then he died, or rather was killed by a bus mounting a pavement when the driver had a heart attack at the wheel. Perhaps Sebastian inherited his affinity for disaster from Father.

Talking of fathers, Andy isn't coming till next weekend now. Kate's feeling low, so Mother's taking her on a shopping spree to Plymouth tomorrow. Selena, Sebastian and I are quite certain we can manage the baby between us for a day but we can see that Kate believes some disaster will befall.

KIDNEY: an organ in the body designed for filtering impurities out of the blood. Also the name given to those large red beans, because of their similarity in shape, I suppose.

Selena had left a bowl of these beans soaking over-

145

night in the kitchen and Sebastian knocked them over while he was making coffee in the early hours of the morning. While probably not being enough noise to wake a sleeping person, this caused sufficient commotion to decide me, lying half awake anyway, to investigate. There are people who express surprise at the courage or foolishness of going to investigate noises in the night, but with our present *ménage* there must be more danger from within than without, and any burglar would be well advised to make his departure while he may. Anyway, the kitchen light was on, and burglars don't go around switching lights on.

I was still feeling sleepy as I stumbled down the stairs but was soon jerked awake by the sight of Sebastian, draped in a scarcely concealing flowered negligee, scrabbling around on the floor scooping up handfuls of wet kidney beans and smashed earthenware and depositing them in the washing up bowl. Joey stood looking on transfixed, and the air slowly filled with steam from the fast-boiling kettle. I switched off the kettle and sat down, fascinated by the sight of Sebastian's man-sized organ drooping below the frills of the negligee. His naked body was nothing new to me, of course, but as he grew up I'd seen it less and less often and had not really been aware of the full implications of its development.

'Oh come on, Mum, give us a hand,' he begged.

'What on earth are you doing?' Guilty, pushing images of penises from my mind, I fell to my knees beside him, picking up a bean or two.

'Isn't it obvious? I'm trying to pick up these ruddy beans.'

'Yes, but what I mean is, how did they get all over the floor?'

'Well I'd like to pretend Joey did it, but that wouldn't be fair. Why did Selena have to leave them so close to the kettle?'

'I expect she doesn't know you well enough yet to allow for you to be rampaging around the kitchen at

146

three in the morning.' I found a pan and brush and a sponge mop and set to work in a more practical manner. 'What are you actually up to, though?'

'Making coffee. Would you like one too?' He set out four cups. 'Come and join the party.'

'What's going on?'

'Commander Forrester's just dropped in, through the window. We asked him to stay for coffee.'

It wasn't making sense. I followed Sebastian, carrying the tray so that he could clutch the negligee around himself. We crept up the stairs along the corridor to the end room that he occupies with Selena. She was sitting up in bed leaning against the wall, all cosy and buxom in a green nightdress, face alight with smiles. The only sign of her disability was the wheelchair in the corner of the room. Sitting on a stool near the window was Commander Forrester, who looked rather shamefaced when he saw me. Sebastian got back into bed, where he was less exposed, and sat close to Selena. I had to sit on the end of the bed.

'I found Mum in the kitchen,' Sebastian explained.

'Do you often have these night experiences?' I asked, still uncertain as to what was going on.

'Not like tonight,' Selena said. 'Someone tell her or I shall start laughing again and spill my coffee. Oh, your face, your face! I shall never forget!'

Between this stifled laughter and blushes from the Commander, I learned that Sebastian and Selena had been copulating rather energetically when without warning the Commander had leapt through the open window onto their bed.

'The curtains were drawn. I couldn't see it was the wrong couple until I was halfway through and by that time it was too late . . .'

'Who did you think it was?'

'It sounded like Gabby. She's rather noisy, you know.'

'Let's see, you jumped through the window because you thought . . .' I suddenly realized that we were on the first floor and quickly visualized the outside of that end of the cottage. 'Wait a minute, you actually climbed a drainpipe in order to leap through the window because you thought Gabby was having it off with Sebastian?'

'Oh, I didn't stop to work out who she might be with. I just wanted . . . well, I don't know what I wanted. I was angry. I'm sorry. That's what jealousy does for you.'

'You've a right to be angry.'

'But I'm not usually, you see. We've got on fine up to now, with the help of my Nelson eye and a bit of generosity of spirit. But since I fell out with you all last week it's been building up rather, all sorts of little things have been niggling me, and then I discovered that this foreign chap who's been lodging with us is one of your lot too . . .'

'Didn't you know?'

'Why should I? No one told me. I thought he seemed a bit eccentric but there was no other reason to connect him with you. Then this evening I find Gabby crying, saying Sven's gone back to his wife and I say Oh, then he's found her has he, where is she? And she tells me he's known where she was all along, she's your sister. Well I don't mind telling you I was pretty angry with him for taking advantage of Gabby and not being straightforward with me and I decided he had to go, but Gabby told me he'd already gone, and then she went too.'

This was a little worrying. Up to going to bed we'd seem no sign of either Gabby or Sven. Supposing they'd run away together? The Commander stared sadly into his coffee cup, embarrassment forgotten as he remembered other emotions. A silence was on the room. Sebastian's arm had slipped around Selena's shoulders. He had sat like that in my bed once, small and cuddly in a checked dressing-gown, my arm around him and a bear or two enjoying the intimacy.

'I really can't apologize enough to these two young people,' the Commander finally said rather awkwardly. 'I mean, so rude.'

'And illegal too, climbing through people's windows in the middle of the night,' I suggested.

'I know, I know. You'd be quite within your rights if you'd called the police. You see, I'd been sitting and drinking alone ever since Gabby rushed off and I really wasn't myself at all.'

'Instead of drinking alone why not carry on coming round here in the evenings? You apologize to Mother and we won't mention this little incident.'

'Really? Blackmail, eh?'

'Bargaining.'

'Well, put it like that . . . I must say I have missed you all rather.'

Coffee was finished and it was time to go back to our respective beds and leave searching for missing people until the morning. After all, their whereabouts was academic; they couldn't actually have come to any harm. But just then we were startled by a ruffling of the curtains and the rattling of several pebbles onto the wooden floor. A second salvo landed before any of us really understood what was happening. This was the only lighted window in the house and someone outside wanted our attention. I looked out cautiously and saw Sven staring up from the path. 'Please come to let me in, Sally. I think I have broken my arm. I fell off the roof.'

'But where's Gabby?' asked the Commander at my elbow. 'Is she still up there?'

'Gabby was not on the roof. I was alone. She I saw walking along the beach with Mr Potter.'

It was the outhouse roof he'd fallen off, trying to get into Julia's room to effect a reconciliation in the manner of the dark clad athletes who deliver the chocolate boxes. I woke Julia and suggested that she might drive him to the hospital. It made a wonderful difference to their relationship. I don't quite know where they patched it up but they managed it somehow, even with Sven's arm in plaster.

*　　*　　*

149

KISMET: fate. Who's to say? More convenient than blaming ourselves or each other.

KISS: a touching with the lips as an expression of love. I have read that the kiss originated when mothers used to masticate their babies' food in their own mouths and then pass it to the mouth of the infant. As some species of animals and birds feed their young by similar methods this may very well be true. It is certain that for most of us the first kisses we receive are from our mothers and these are the first kisses we learn to return. Later we long to be kissed by a stranger of the opposite sex, most of us, and the kiss becomes part of the vocabulary of erotic sexual foreplay. This transformation of the innocent to the erotic is something I find difficult to handle. I like Selena and I know Sebastian's a grown-up person, and I don't actually mind about them having a relationship. What bothers me is that I can't get used to the idea. I keep on thinking about it, and I also keep on thinking about what Sebastian wrote to Pope. If I'm having difficulty, how must it have been for a child? And for God's sake no wonder there are mother-in-law problems!

KNIFE: a sharp-bladed implement used for cutting, usually food, but sometimes people. This must be a gory and painful procedure, though I believe it happens quite often among some sections of the population, and of course every day in hospitals in the name of medicine.

But people can cut each other up metaphorically too, without the actual use of cold steel or the sight of blood, and the effects can be even more painful and enduring. As when Bruce received confirmation about his appointment in Sunderland and read it out at breakfast. No, it wasn't the appointment that caused me pain. In fact I was pleased and congratulated him on it. 'When will you be making the move?'

'I have to start in the autumn. If we both give in our notice by next week we could get moved up there in the summer.'

150

'We? Both?'

He looked at me as though I was stupid, in much the same way as Pope does sometimes. 'Well, yes, of course. The two of us, and Sebastian.'

'But I work here, and Sebastian's got his exams.'

'You'll easily get another job, specially if I'm in charge.'

'But I've got my research project set up for next term; you know, the family therapy study. I want to use it to write up my doctorate, then I can apply to have my own department.'

'Oh come on, Sally, you know that's pie in the sky. You're not up to it. You couldn't sustain the concentration long enough. Stick to what you do best. You're a good thorough lecturer and I can easily get you a post in my new department.'

'Have you thought that I might not want just another lecturer's job, and especially not because of the favours of one of the appointing academics?'

'What's wrong with that? It was good enough for you last time.'

'What do you mean?'

'Pope giving you your job because he wanted to help you.'

'I got that job because I was the best applicant.'

'That's not what he said to me.'

KNIT: a method of interlocking yarn into a flat fabric. It's a total mystery to me how it's done. I watch with admiration when people clack and waggle those needles together and produce a lengthening strip of garment, often covered with intricate patterns. Nobody knits much in our family, except Selena.

14   Laughter—Lust

Life is littered with lovely Ls, like love and laughter and lollipops and luck. There are also some that are not so good, like lice and laziness and lust. All of which are fraught with problems, and if you think lollipops and lice are pretty straightforward then you haven't lived in a house with five children, a dog and two guinea-pigs. Apart from both beginning with an L they share the propensity to get everywhere, once embarked. Even after the children had been liberally treated with some tactfully packaged special shampoo that was frightfully difficult to lather, the adults jumped nervously at every sign of an itch or prickle for days afterwards. This nervous jump would be followed by a quick glance around to see if anyone else had noticed, then a furtive scratching followed by a discreet dash from the room, no doubt to make a thorough inspection. The fact that only half a dozen lice had been found, and those only on Roger, who liked to sleep with Joey alongside him, didn't prevent the incident from receiving the same attention as a major epidemic of some incurable disease, nor prevent Kate from openly accusing Potter of being the cause.

'No chance m'dear,' said Potter, happily filling his face with bacon and eggs. 'Fleas can't swim and I bathe in the sea every day.' That would account for that salt-encrusted look he has.

'So does Roger but that didn't keep them off him.'

'Not so thoroughly, Missus. He's inclined to go in tippy toe and not put his head under water unless a wave catches him. I know, I've watched him. And you know the waves are very small this fine weather.' Kate couldn't answer that because she just didn't know. She rarely went near the beach as it was too far for her to walk in her still delicate state.

Lollipops? Well, Selena makes lollipops, many different flavours, in the freezer, so the children can help themselves whenever the fancy takes them. The trouble is that they also abandon them whenever and wherever their fancy is diverted elsewhere, such as on kitchen chairs, in the bathroom, on the verandah table. These soon become sticky pools of brightly coloured liquid that appear to contain very strong dye. 'Hell,' muttered Sebastian, scrubbing with scouring powder at the side of the bath, 'If it does this to enamel what must it do to their insides?'

LAUGHTER: I really should have begun with this. I can only describe it as a strange and noisy catching of the breath, not unlike a hiccup, which afflicts humans when they are very happy or greatly amused. This description does nothing to convey the actual experience which is generally quite involuntary and overwhelming, although it can be directed so as to appear at socially expected moments, such as when a commedien(ne) has delivered a joke. Often, though, it appears at unexpected moments, quite out of context, which can be embarrassing both for the laugher and the laughed at. It tends to be most gripping and uncontrollable at those moments.

LAZINESS: an inclination not to work. I have always thought of Sebastian as lazy until now, which I suppose was unjust. He simply didn't want to do the things I thought he ought to be doing. Looking back, I realize he was always busy at something: reading things, planting things, causing havoc. Now that he's endlessly busy about the place and it seems to be well-directed energy, I can see he's not lazy and I'm satisfied.

* * *

LETTER: one of the symbols of the alphabet, of which our language has twenty-six, so at L I'm less than half way through. And yet since Sebastian and Selena have been running the household I've been able to get on so fast with my actual thesis that I've practically finished the first draft.

A letter is also a written form of communication between two people distanced from each other. After he left us Bruce used to write, mostly to Sebastian but sometimes to me, telling me how impressive he was being in his new job, and how lonely he was without us, and repeating his suggestion that I would be happy married to him.

Yes, married!

He did make a proposal before he left but in a way that I found totally resistible. It came about when he was packing his books and Sebastian, suspicious of the heavy silence of the past few weeks, came to ask me when we'd be packing our things.

'We're not going,' I said, trying to make it sound natural and unimportant.

Sebastian's face whitened. 'Well you do what you want,' he said, 'but I'm going with Bruce.'

I would have laughed if he'd been six instead of sixteen. 'Darling, you have your exams to take and I've got my job.'

'What do they matter if Bruce goes away? Life will be just awful. I want to go with him.'

'But you don't belong to him.' Bruce came to the doorway, his face as strained as Sebastian's.

'I would if you were married. Why can't you two be married? Married people go together.'

'That's it,' Bruce said slowly. 'That's what you want, isn't it? Why don't we get married?'

There was a time when I would have readily agreed, before he'd made those remarks about my job and my capabilities. But nothing had been the same after that. Each day had passed in a limbo of empty anger. I wanted nothing so much as not to have him around any more. So I said, 'No, not for either of you,' and thereby crushed the one I loved together with the one I hated.

Sebastian cried when Bruce left. He didn't speak to me for weeks. He stopped working for his exams and went back onto the dope. I told myself he would get over it and got on with my work.

LOCALITY: the place around one, or around whatever is being talked about; the adjacent physical scene. Which brings my mind back to the worry of the Commander's disappearance.

Despite his promise to carry on with his early evening social calls, he didn't appear. He was at home the following night, though Gabby can't remember him speaking to her but put it down to temporary huffiness because she'd stayed out most of the night. He was spotted around the village once or twice during the following day and then it seemed he just locked up the house and went away. He didn't take his car, he didn't catch the bus (unless he was in disguise) and wasn't seen thumbing a lift. You see, we made very thorough enquiries. After Gabby had come to us for help we had a lengthy conference around the kitchen table. We felt rather deeply involved, not least because Gabby had been locked out of her home and our roof was the nearest alternative she had. The Commander had been so thorough that it was impossible to break in. Every window was locked and shuttered from within, every door bolted and mortised. Short of doing major damage there was no way in. It's difficult to know whether Gabby was more distraught at being cut off from her possessions than at having lost her husband. In the end, fearing a suicide attempt, mother called the police, who smashed in a side door with an axe.

'I could have done that,' Potter commented as we stood and watched.

'You'd have spoiled their fun,' I said.

155

'And got arrested for it,' Sebastian pointed out.

Gabby and the two policemen vanished through the wrecked door and from the outside we could see lights coming on in one room after another behind the shutters. Finally the front door was opened and we were given the news that there was no sign of the Commander. This was a relief because I had been conjuring up pictures of a stiffening corpse being found somewhere. After the policemen departed, Mother suggested that Gabby could come and stay with us rather than spend the night alone in that big house but she declined, which was perfectly understandable since it was unlikely that she would be alone for more than half an hour after we'd all cleared off. In fact, we left Sebastian and Potter making a temporary repair to the smashed door, and Sebastian later came back alone, so there wasn't even any need for face-saving explanations.

LOTTERY: a form of gambling where you invest your money in a ticket which may or may not win you a prize. I became involved in this rather against my will at the Cricket Club fête. The Commander had undertaken to run something called a bottle stall but because he wasn't there someone had to do it for him, and as Mother was involved with cakes, and Selena and Sebastian were selling flowers, I agreed to help out. Only then did I discover that I had to spend the morning rushing around the village begging full bottles of one sort or another from all the members of the Cricket Club and any other likely supporters; then stick half raffle tickets on them. Then I had to fold up the other halves of dozens and dozens of raffle tickets into a biscuit tin, making sure that there were many more tickets than there were bottles so that every dip into the tin, which had to be paid for, did not result in a bottle being won. I couldn't imagine this being much of a success but I was wrong. The fête was held on the edge of the cricket field at the same time as a limited-overs match was being

156

played. Players, players' families, villagers and visitors gathered around just for the purpose of spending money without appearing to be interested in gaining anything useful. During the tea break Mother, very dashing in her red linen boiler suit, judged the cakes. They were anonymously presented to her and she regained quite a lot of good will by declaring Nancy's chocolate sponge to have won first prize. Then the entries were quickly auctioned before the sun turned them into unmanageable blobs of runny butter icing and sour cream. Gabby's worries didn't put her off her game, so the cricket team scored another sound victory and a successful afternoon was had by all. The only unsatisfied person was the publican's wife who had bought a number of the cakes, at some expense, in order to impress her neighbours with her generosity. She intended to stow these away in her freezer for future use but she left them in a cardboard box under the trestle table for a few moments while she wandered over to the flower stall and became engaged in a lengthy conversation with Selena. In the meantime Joey, hopelessly tempted by the smell and unable to believe his luck, scoffed most of the contents of the box.

One can't exactly shoot a dog for savaging cream cakes, and as the money was for charity the poor woman didn't like to ask for it back. I tried to smooth over the situation by giving her a bottle of wine from my stall that the minimarket had donated, and only realized later that a bottle of wine to a publican's wife must be like a sleigh ride to Santa Claus. Joey, when he understood he had done wrong, set off home at a swift gallop and was sick all over the back doorstep.

LOVE: a much maligned attachment. I mean, love is supposed to be caring for other people and I have always liked to think that means being more interested in the welfare of another person than in your own welfare, rather than wanting to have a person with you for the good that person can do to you. I know it feels as though you love a person or a place if it hurts to be without them but I'm not sure that attachment is anything other than self love.

Bruce would write, 'I love you, Sally, and I want you to be with me here,' when he must have known that I would only be unhappy even to hear that, let alone to comply. And Sebastian said one day, 'If you loved me you'd marry Bruce to make me happy.' Tricky one, that. So I don't love Bruce because I won't sacrifice myself to be with him and that seems acceptable, if hard headed. But it also seems that I don't love Sebastian because I won't sacrifice myself for his interests, which isn't nearly so easy to live with. I very nearly swallowed it and gave in but the instinct for self-preservation is strong, particularly supported by the reasoning that in a very few years Sebastian would grow up and go away and I would be left as a dissatisfied academic wife, doing a second choice job that I only held because of my husband's position. No thank you.

Talking of love, Sven and Julia are now enjoying a brief second honeymoon on the Isles of Scilly. Mother drove them to Penzance to catch the flight.

LUCK: fortune or chance, meant to be good unless it's deliberately prefaced with the word 'bad'. Some people say there is no such thing as luck; the things that happen to us, good or bad, come about through our own doing. But if that's true it's difficult to explain the chance that has brought us all together here during this fine weather, which has certainly shaped events. For instance, if the sun hadn't been shining the children wouldn't have been outdoors so much; wouldn't have met Potter; wouldn't have dug up the lawn. Mother wouldn't have been out sailing or power-boating, Sven wouldn't have spent time on the hillside, at least I don't think he would. The summer would have been dominoes and cards and trips to the cinema instead, and a longer employment for Joan and Nancy and Jennifer, who incidentally asked after us all quite wistfully at the fête.

And Sebastian and Selena were lucky, too, with each other. They needed a bit of luck, after all. I said this to Sebastian as we shared the washing up, watching through the window as Selena gave Stevie rides along the path on her wheelchair. 'You were lucky to meet up with her,' wondering as I said it how many mothers would call it luck to find their sons emotionally attached to a girl in a wheelchair.

Sebastian nodded. 'I could have been another year at the centre if it hadn't been for Selena. You know, at the first session when we were put together I felt really bad about being with her and I tried to hide it so as not to be bawled out by the therapists, and Selena said, "You feel really bad about this, don't you?" and I said, "Yes" and she said we should ask to be reassigned because she didn't fancy the look of me much either. Then I asked her what was the point of fancying anyone anyway when you couldn't have sex and she said she'd show me sometime.'

'What a way to begin!'

'Yeah, wasn't it? Then I thought I'd been a bit hard on her and I began to feel sorry for her. First time I slept with her it was just to be nice to her. And you know she really took me over, it was like nothing else, and I couldn't bear to be away from her after that.'

LUNATIC: somebody mad, unhinged. This definition arises from the belief that mad people stared at the moon, or that people who stared at the moon became mad, perhaps.

It can be argued that there's no such thing as madness, just different perceptions of sanity. That same logic can also be applied to what is meant by normality, which leads me to believe that there needn't necessarily be anything odd about me because I didn't want to marry a brilliant man on his way up in the world.

But Bruce didn't see it that way. He came to London

159

for a conference about a year after we'd parted and visited us. He was wearing a suit and he'd cut his hair and his conversation was more pompous than funny. Even Sebastian was disappointed. He stayed the night, and we slept together and I was surprised at what a smooth and practised lover he seemed, or had I just forgotten? I couldn't abandon myself to this confident and dominating person. From the moment we started I only wanted it to stop. So I felt guilty because I didn't have to have been there and it wasn't his fault I didn't want to be invaded. Afterwards he said, 'My God, Sally, why can't you be more normal? Don't you think you ought to see a psychiatrist?'

LUST: greed, mainly in a sexual context. Many people interpret this drive to possess another person as love, and there is some connection as lust does on occasion lead to love and I suppose it works the other way round too.

At lunchtime today Sven and Julia hobbled out of the taxi which had brought them all the way from Penzance. They now have to face the problem of how to take two cars back to Sweden when only one of them is fit to drive.

In the late afternoon Andy's car drew up. He has really arrived to take his family home at last, and gloom has settled on the household.

15 Macassar—Mother

MACASSAR: a kind of hair oil from an island in the Indian Ocean that became very popular with the Victorians, who apparently admired a smooth head of hair. Unfortunately this oil soaks into any fabric it comes into contact with, which caused problems with the backs of armchairs, showing that a great many Victorian gentle men seemed to sit around in armchairs. So the Victorian housewife took to making embroidered linen covers to put on chairbacks, it being easier to launder a length of linen regularly than an armchair. These 'anti-macassars' also had the advantage of covering up shabby chairs and of cutting down the spread of head lice, or so it was believed. What seems remarkable about all this is that these women meekly embroidered and laundered endlessly rather than getting together to ban the use of the horrid oil, as I'm sure would happen nowadays.

MANAGEMENT: the organization of work. This word is also used as a collective noun to refer to the group of people at the top who run an outfit. There are those who say that management shouldn't be in the hands of a few individuals but should be conducted by consensus of all the workers involved. I can see problems in this as a consensus can often lead to a bland compromise, a situation where nobody is pleased and nothing is done. But at least it would avoid the kind of problems I've found myself facing as a member of a department managed by Professor Pope.

I first became aware that I had a problem when I applied for Bruce's post after he left. I suppose I'd been too confident of getting it, having the experience, and having set up the family therapy research project. I was interviewed, but it didn't go well. Pope kept turning the questions away from my work to relationships with colleagues and imputing that I was difficult to get along with. The job was finally given to Meg, younger than me with a glib tongue and high qualifications. I sulked and smarted but was soon able to rejoice quietly when she began to suggest radical changes in policy that made things difficult for Pope. Then he tried to wind up my project and transfer my research assistants to another job, but I fought that one and got outside funding and began to publish some of my findings in the journals. You see, I'd realized that if I was to get a promotion anywhere else I'd need supporting references of a kind that I wasn't likely to get from Pope. I was encouraged by Meg. 'This is fine work, Sally. You explain things very well. Some researchers can't put two sentences together without wandering off the point. I sometimes wonder about our dear Professor. Do you know his wife corrects all his papers as she types them?'

It was Meg who helped me to find the names and addresses of the treatment centres I tried to get Sebastian to go to.

MOAT: a wide ditch around a castle, filled with water, to make invasion more difficult.

Our own wet ditch is having to be filled in. We had a letter from the Parish Council indicating that they were rather annoyed about water being diverted from the stream. Potter thinks they have no legal case but since the water level is now so low that there's only a small trickle, Sebastian has started a filling in job. A pity because he'd made it look so nice.

*　　*　　*

MOTHER: the bearer of off-spring, female parent, nurturer of a family.

Kate wants to go home. She wants to go back to the security of her own house, where she is in control, with Andy and her pretty children all in a predictable situation. Now that she's been made certain of Andy's intentions by his presence among us, she's rushing around the place packing for real. Relays of small, glum porters carry packages out to the enormous car, to be stowed by Andy, ready for departure tomorrow.

Andy is jolly and determined, playing the role of happy dad and not even blinking when he encounters Gabby, calling in to make her daily report on the non-appearance of the Commander. The rest of us are going about our business rather more quietly than usual, nobody liking to admit that we don't want the children to go.

Sven has hit on the idea of finding some impoverished hitch-hiker to drive his car back to Sweden in return for remuneration and an air fare home, and has set off to scour the village for such a person. Julia says he's being stupid and impractical; even if he does find someone willing to undertake the journey, how are they to know the car won't be crashed or stolen? Sven thinks this is a risk worth taking since a car in Cornwall, even in one piece, is useless to them in Uppsala. Thus they have had their first quarrel since their reunion.

With the heat and the gloom, activity had wound down to a crawl by mid-afternoon and one by one we all gathered on the shady side of the verandah, except Kate who was still packing. The children draped themselves over the steps, even Stevie who wasn't accustomed to being still, but who had worked out by then that one way of being included in the activities of his elders was to imitate them unremittingly. Joey was uneasy and kept circling the cottage to sniff around the car which he knew, with the unerring good sense of all dogs, was soon to play a key part in the disruption of his life. Gabby

163

twittered on in a desultory way about the locked house and her husband's apparently callous disappearance.

Just as Andy was saying, not for the first time, that he didn't think there'd be room in the car for a box of guinea-pigs and a dog, a commotion of squealing and barking broke out around the corner leading to the drive. The children jumped up to investigate and arrived just in time to see Joey munching the hindquarters of the last guinea-pig. The ensuing pandemonium was memorable for cries such as, 'How did they get out?' 'It isn't fair! It isn't fair!' 'There's nothing left even to stuff!' 'Not both of them, surely?' 'Who opened the cage?' 'But he wasn't hungry!'

Kate's appearance at the back door was greeted by a unified verbal attack from the three eldest children (Stevie was bawling to himself in loud and uncontrollable grief), who screamed varying versions of, 'You were the only person we couldn't see and we all know you hated them! You let them out when Joey was around so we'd lose the guinea-pigs and hate Joey too! Well it hasn't worked. You can't pin a crime on a dog like that. We still love him and we hate you!' Kate sat down on the edge of the ramp and burst into tears and Roger, Amelia and Miranda fled along the lane with Joey. Andy started after them, then decided that his duty lay with Kate. Muttering, 'Is there no sense of order in this place? No wonder you're so keen to go home, my darling,' he put his arms around his sobbing wife and guided her inside and upstairs.

Mother comforted Stevie who had tried to make his escape with the others but been restrained by Sebastian before he reached the gate. Selena went in and put the kettle on and I helped her to prepare a tray of tea.

As we regrouped on the verandah Julia asked, 'Oughtn't we to organize a search party or something?'

'Or tell the police?' suggested Sven.

'They won't go far,' Mother assured us. 'Children never do.'

164

I didn't share her belief on that point, despite her superior experience. Most children might creep back home after dark and a missed meal, but not these. They would manage to eat somehow and darkness and cold weren't likely to worry them. With their resourcefulness the possibilities were universal. Long distance lorries, ocean liners: they might end up anywhere. But the police wouldn't be interested until they'd missed a couple of meals, and with the area full of tourists where should we begin to look?

We progressed from tea to gin and tonic. Gabby went to look for the Commander, again with no luck. Andy and Kate didn't reappear. The baby cried and Selena fed him. Stevie snoozed on the hammock. Sebastian dug. Then Potter came ambling through the hedge and across the lawn and we all knew, with a mutual spark of inspiration, that here was the man who would know how to find the children.

Actually he didn't need to give the matter any thought because he already knew where they were. That was why he came back so early. He'd seen them scrambling up the cliffs to the smugglers' caves and begin to build a barricade of rocks across the top of the path. We gave him a gin and tonic while we explained what had happened. He's stuck to cider most of his life, except during his seafaring years, but Mother has coaxed him into this new taste which he's embraced with enthusiasm, now consuming gin in almost the same quantity as he did cider.

'If they've barricaded themselves in we can starve them out,' Mother suggested.

'No Ma'am,' Potter said gently. 'There's enough chocolate and crêpes and pâté in them caves to keep them going quite a while. Unless they get cold they can last out for weeks.'

'That could be inconvenient.'

'It could ruin my trade. But I think I know the answer.' We all brightened up. 'A barbecue.'

'Human sacrifice?' I asked.

'Child or parent?' Gabby queried.

'A beach barbecue,' Potter went on, having learned to ignore us if it suited his flow. 'A farewell party. All their friends and family, music and dancing and the smell of sausages and steak.'

We caught onto the idea quite quickly and liked it too. Selena and Mother went off to organize the food, Gabby thought she could round up some supporters and find help with the music through her Cricket Club contacts and the rest of us went down to the beach to build a driftwood bonfire. Andy came to help us later on but Kate thought we'd all gone quite mad and said she would boycott the proceedings.

By the time it was dark we had a sizeable fire already kindled and, as well as half the Cricket Club and their families, a great many interested holiday-makers drifted in our direction from their after-supper walks. Sebastian and Andy raked the embers at the edge of the fire and set up cooking grills. Potter came down from the pub carrying two flagons of cider. Up on the cliff side a small light flickered into a tiny rival fire. I thought it was a bit much to expect unconditional surrender and that someone should go and talk to them but Andy disagreed. He believed that uncertainty was the essence of suffering and he intended to punish his children. So I set off up the narrow path which was luckily well lit by the beach bonfire. The children had made an efficient job of their barricade, but when they saw it was me they removed a few key stones and allowed me into their cave. Joey wagged his tail, pleased to see me.

'You're missing your farewell party,' I told them.

'We didn't know there was going to be one.'

'It's Potter's surprise.'

'We're sorry about that but we're not coming down.'

'Not ever?'

'Not ever.' Then Miranda admitted, 'We will on condition that we can have some more guinea-pigs when we get home.'

166

'And that we can take Joey with us.'

'And that we won't get punished for running away.'

'Or for what we said to Mum.'

'Yeah, we're sorry about that, but we were upset.'

'A lot of conditions,' I said. 'It's a bit steep.'

'Well do they want us back or not?'

'Your mother isn't down there. How can your father make promises he knows she wouldn't like?'

'He can persuade her about anything if he wants.'

'Anyway we won't come down otherwise and then they can't take us home.'

'No punishments,' Andy agreed. 'But no animals either.'

'They won't go home without that dog, Andy.'

'They'll have to. I won't have my car invaded by hairs and smells, and Kate feels the same about the carpets and furniture. No dog. And I thought I said no negotiations.'

'You might just end up with no children.'

'They'll come down eventually. Really Sally, I don't see that you can claim to be an expert in dealing with children.'

I carried the message to the children who were resigned and unmoved. 'Pity,' said Roger. 'It looks a good party.' Unfortunately for them Joey thought so too. He was bored with sitting in a cave while so much interesting activity was going on below so he set off down the path, ignoring the despairing commands from above. After a short conference the children decided that Joey might well disappear for ever if they weren't there to keep an eye on him and his life was more important than their principles. They put out their defiant little fire and we all scrambled down to the beach together.

I had thought it might be a good idea to avoid Andy for a while but Joey immediately singled him out as the most important person on the beach and the one who just had to be licked and jostled before all others. As he was chatting up Gabby at the time his dignity was undermined and he needed to be reminded that he had promised no punishments. The children pulled Joey away, breathless and apprehensive. 'Savages!' he muttered.

'Aren't you pleased to have us back?' Miranda asked soothingly.

'Just keep that dog out of the way, then I'll decide.'

'Where's some food?' asked Roger. 'Surely they've kept some food for us?'

'Go and see Sebastian or Granny.'

But Granny was dancing with a very merry Potter and Sebastian was sitting in the sea with an arm around Selena, watching the growing groups of people who had sensibly decided to take off most of their clothes and have a night swim. Sebastian and Selena were not among the sensible, being still fully dressed so that their wet clothes grotesquely accentuated their bodies. They rolled against each other, laughing helplessly. I cooked a pan of sausages for the children.

Although there was no moon there was enough light from the stars for everyone to see the long dark shape and tall mast of the *Rialto* as it rounded the headland and glided to a standstill off from the beach. The sound of the engine was hidden under the noise of our music so there was something ghostly about the movement of the darkened boat without a single sail raised. We saw a glint and a slight splash as an anchor was dropped, then a few moments later the trailing dinghy was pulled in and a figure climbed down into it and began to row towards us. By that time the dancing and bathing had stopped and we all stood watching, half in and half out of the water. The music tape came to its end and, except for the lapping of water and the steady squeak and dip of oars, silence enveloped the scene.

A silence broken by one of the children as the dinghy came into the shallow water. 'It's the Commander!' And they rushed forward to grab the bows and steady the boat onto the beach.

'Oh good!' Mother stepped unsteadily forward. 'So nice to see you, Commander. So glad you could come to our little farewell party.'

He stood upright and stepped ashore with all the stuffy dignity of an eighteenth-century sea captain making a landing amongst a crowd of naked savages. But instead of saying, 'I claim this land for King George,' he said, 'I've just bought the *Rialto* and I'm looking for a crew to take her across the Atlantic.'

He had judged the situation beautifully. Gabby ran down the beach and flung her arms around him, kissing him passionately over and over again. 'Why didn't you say what you were planning?' she cried. 'Please take me! Oh thank God you're all right! I was so worried about you!'

'Just as you are,' he said. 'We're sailing tonight.'

'The Atlantic? Oh boy!' Mother muttered, eyes glazed, clambering into the dinghy.

Miranda, Rog, Melly and Joey stood in a half circle around the bow of the dinghy, staring wistfully but sensing that here was something beyond them.

'Any more, any more?' cried the Commander, his arm round Gabby's waist. He might well have been joined by one or two inebriated tourists but just then someone put more wood on the fire and changed the tape in the player, and the scene around the dinghy became part of just another make-believe local pageant to all except those most closely concerned.

'Try a sup of this first,' said Potter, handing the Commander a cider flagon from which he managed to swallow several large gulps without spilling a drop.

'What about you, Potter? You're a seafaring man. Be proud to have you in my crew.'

'Thank you, Commander, but no. I've my own interests to attend to.'

A slight ruffling of the atmosphere made me aware that Kate was striding towards us along the beach, wearing slacks and cardigan and possessed of all her old confidence and determination. 'Whatever's going on here?' she demanded. 'Really Andy, have you no sense of responsibility? It's past eleven o'clock and these children should be in bed. We've got to make an early start in the morning.'

Andy was at that moment trying to negotiate Mother out of the dinghy and being repulsed with sharp slaps on his hands and wrists and cries of, 'Leave me alone, you great oaf!' At the sight of Kate he abandoned his efforts and ran to her side. 'What are you doing here? You shouldn't have walked all that way.'

'I didn't, you idiot, I drove round. And just as well too. Otherwise the children would have been forced to witness you assaulting their grandmother. Now bring them home at once and let Sally sort things out here.'

Kate meant what she said about the early start. I was woken next morning by the sounds of breakfasting children and the final packing of the car and I dressed and joined them, wondering if there was going to be a showdown about Joey. But the dog was nowhere to be seen and nobody mentioned it, which was suspicious in itself. The children were bleary-eyed and in no state to oppose any command from their parents, who were exercising full authority now that a calm and orderly environment was within their grasp.

When she had packed the final Thermos flask into the picnic bag, Kate looked around the dish-strewn kitchen and said, 'Do you mind if we leave the washing up, Sally? I expect Sebastian and Selena will do it.' Then, 'I did hope Mother would be up to see us off but Andy thinks she must have rather a hangover. Sally, you will look after her, won't you? She isn't young any more, you know. What time did she get to bed in the end?'

I avoided confessing that I didn't know by offering to carry the picnic bag out. I had left the party soon after Kate and Andy and had gone for a walk before going home. Perhaps I should have stayed to sort things out but I didn't see it as my business to interfere any further. If Mother wanted to go on the razzle why should I try to stop her?

170

With a minimum of further ado the Randolphs were packed up into the car and Sven and Julia appeared in time to say goodbye. Potter hove round the corner of the cottage just as the engine started, but no Mother. 'We won't disturb her,' Andy decided. 'We'll phone when we get home.' As they slowly turned out of the gate the sad, sunbrowned little faces all turned for a last look and a wave.

Sven was busy making phone calls to an insurance company. At the beach party he had found a carefree wanderer willing and able to take his car home for him and needed to make arrangements quickly. It seemed to be everybody's day for going home. As Julia packed I sat in the kitchen with Potter and drank coffee. I suddenly noticed that the sky was clouded over not with the fine mist of many past mornings but with a heavy layer of grey.

Potter looked pale under his suntan and moved slowly. Once he moaned gently. 'I can drink all the cider in the world but it just don't mix with gin.' he observed.

'You're not the only one who knows that this morning.'

'How did you escape then?'

'I was too busy climbing up and down the cliff and cooking sausages.' Thank goodness. 'Where's Joey?'

'On his way eastwards.'

'No? How come?'

'In the car, with the kids.'

'No, he wasn't. You saw them go as well as I did. No dog there.'

'No dog anywhere else, m'dear.'

This was true. 'How did they manage it? And how do you know about it?'

'I helped them repack the suitcases at crack of dawn, and give the dog a sup of brandy to make it sleep. He stowed away real nice.'

No wonder the silence. I tried to imagine what would happen when Andy found out. Mayhem? Submission? Death? Perhaps a move towards greater understanding and family harmony? I went upstairs and began to work. The cottage was blissfully quiet. My mind locked into total concentration which was only disturbed at lunchtime by Sven calling up from the drive, 'We go now, Sally, Mother, everyone. Thank you for looking after us!'

I felt obliged to go down and wave them off. The two expensive sports cars left in convoy, one of them driven by a penniless young man who still couldn't believe his luck.

The quietness of the house was beginning to disturb me. I crept to Sebastian and Selena's room and opened the door a crack, and found it unoccupied. I remembered I'd last seen them sitting in the sea together but surely they must have moved from there? Or someone must have moved them. Perhaps they had fallen asleep on the beach. Then I went to Mother's room and found a similar lack of person. I had last seen Mother volunteering to crew for a voyage across the Atlantic. It was then that I became seriously worried.

Potter was asleep on the hammock and none too easy to wake. He was irritable at my questions. Yes, of course he knew where they were. He'd shoved them all off from the beach.

'All?'

'Sure enough. A right overloaded boat what with the wheelchair having to go along too.'

'He took Mother and Sebastian and Selena?'

'I wouldn't say he so much took them as they went along. After all, it's a fine opportunity for someone with no responsibilities. I felt quite tempted myself.'

'They all went off without telling me?'

He wasn't so irritable now. 'They did look for you to go along with them, I distinctly remember that. But they couldn't find you and the Commander wanted to catch the tide. There wasn't much time.'

I couldn't believe it. All gone and left me on my own. When would I ever see them again?

'Don't fret,' Potter soothed. 'They'll be in Falmouth by

now sleeping off their hangovers. They've got to take on stores and equipment for a long trip. Have sense. You'll be hearing from them in a few hours.'

He was right. I went to Falmouth the next day expecting them to return shamefacedly with me, but none of them would be dissuaded from the voyage. They even tried to talk me into going with them. But I thought of long hours cooped up, of rough seas and broken nights and somehow I wasn't gripped by the same spirit of adventure. I could see the attraction of escape, of not having to finish my thesis or face the academic board, of not needing to struggle to establish myself in a new job, of not justifying myself to Pope any more. Adventure versus competition, and I wasn't so much of a fool as to imagine that the adventure would be the most exciting choice. I still needed to retrieve from Pope and Bruce what they had taken from me. After that I wasn't too sure, but I couldn't leave things half finished now.

So I went back to my work while the rain tipped down outside and the earth steamed gently and gave out its rich warm scents. Potter moved his belongings from the outhouse through the summer house to next door, to take up residence as the newly appointed caretaker of the Forresters' property. I donated to him the last case of gin, to see him through the winter. Joan and Nancy were persuaded to come back and spend a few days putting the cottage back in order for its owners and Bassett appeared, uninvited, to finish the job on the lawn.

At the end of the week I paid them, packed my car and departed, leaving them to lock up and look after Mother's car for the winter. By the time they'd tidied up my room the place would be as though we'd never occupied it, yet none of us would ever be the same again.

Epilogue

Zygote

I packed up my thesis for the typist yesterday. I should have done it weeks ago but with the rush of term starting it got delayed. Then I found my Complete Knowledge, still unfinished. I was going to throw it away but perhaps Sebastian would like to read it one day. There must be some significance in the fact that it comes to a stop at MOTHER. I had intended to go right the way through the alphabet and cleverly finish with ZYGOTE, which is a newly fertilized egg, and would take me right back to the beginning again.

Julia phoned yesterday to ask me if I'd like to spend Christmas with them. She's pregnant at last and I suppose she wants me to listen to her talking about babies. This morning a letter arrived from Bermuda saying that they've made the main part of the crossing safely, apart from losing Sebastian overboard about a week ago, but he was on a lifeline so they managed to pick him up quite quickly. I am glad I'm not with them. They plan to be in Jamaica for Christmas and suggested I should fly over and meet them there.

I've also been asked to Kate and Andy's. The children want me to see Joey's puppies when they arrive. No, we didn't make that much of a mistake, but Joey's first adventure after being reprieved and accepted as a full member of the Randolph family was to ravish the bitch next door. I'll go and see them for a weekend, but as this is the first Christmas for a very long time that I haven't had to worry about Sebastian I was thinking of using my holiday to go ski-ing with Meg. I've always wanted to learn to ski.

THE END

The Proprietor
by Ann Schlee

'Written with a subtlety and quiet assurance which is both rare and impressive . . . the kind of novel which makes the prospect of a second reading a pleasure to be savoured'
BOOKS AND BOOKMEN

'Rare and strange . . . rich in detail and steeped in the author's sense of the period and place about which she writes, it establishes Ann Schlee as one of the best new novelists we have'
SUSAN HILL

The islands lay low and dark in the sea that had claimed the lives of Adela Traherne's parents. Known to the islanders as the Island Child, her life became inextricably linked with Augustus Walmer, the Proprietor, in the summer of 1840 when a group of his friends came to see how he was restoring the economy and well-being of his people and the untamed beauty of the islands he owned. None of the people who came together in that summer was ever to forget what happened then, none of them was ever to break free from the islands' grip, and the destinies of Adela and Augustus seemed fated to be forever linked.

'Ambitious, imaginative . . . *The Proprietor* more than a little resembles *The French Lieutenant's Woman,* with a dash of *Jamaica Inn,* and an occasional nod in the direction of *The Waves*'
ANITA BROOKNER, HARPERS & QUEEN

'Outstanding success . . . elegant precision and feeling for period . . . attractive echoes of Charlotte Bronte and Elizabeth Bowen'
HERMIONE LEE, THE OBSERVER

0 552 99099 X   £2.95

BLACK SWAN

The Textures of Silence
Gordon Vorster

'Strong, sensual and vivid, almost tactile . . . a rich and
readable novel'
RAND DAILY MAIL

The Textures of Silence is a remarkable literary achievement, a
powerful affirmation of the potential of life and of man.

At the age of three weeks, Daan Cilliers is critically injured in
an accident that leaves him blind, deaf, dumb and spastic.
Unthinking and unfeeling, he lives in his own world until the
age of fifty, when Maria van der Kolff enters his life. *The
Textures of Silence* is the story of Daan's miraculous rebirth to
awareness and life, but it is also the story of the people around
him and of the forces of love, guilt, passion, endurance, and
knowledge that bring this amazing novel to its triumphant close.

An artist whose paintings are internationally known, an actor
who appeared opposite Athol Fugard in *The Guest*, a producer
and director of both feature and documentary films, Gordon
Vorster is arguably the most versatile creative personality in
South Africa today. With *The Textures of Silence*, he emerges
as a major new novelist to rank alongside Nadine Gordimer,
J.M. Coetzee and Andre Brink.

The Textures of Silence won South Africa's Golden Cape
Award for Fiction.

0 552 99101 5   £3.50

BLACK SWAN